IRYNA BENNETT

Whoever Fights Monsters

Swimming Kangaroo Books, May 2007

Swimming Kangaroo Books

Arlington, Texas

ISBN: 978-1-934041-20-8

LCCN: 2007923421

IRYNA BENNETT

Dive into a good book! Come visit us at

http://www.swimmingkangaroo.com

for a unique reading experience.

IRYNA BENNETT

WHOEVER FIGHTS MONSTERS
by
Iryna Bennett

Swimming Kangaroo Books   Arlington, Texas

IRYNA BENNETT

CHAPTER I

There was blood on the concrete floor, but hardly anything earth shattering.

Detective Mike Reynolds shielded his eyes from the last of the flashes of crime scene photography and downed the rest of his coffee in one gulp. Immediately he wished he hadn't. The coffee was still smoldering-hot, and his tongue was sure to end up with first-degree burns. Another annoyance to go with a two a.m. wake-up call and an altogether rough drive.

"Mike," he heard his name called out in a shrill falsetto. Heather Finley, the youngest field examiner on the force and a notorious insomniac, waved at him from the far end of the spotlight-flooded warehouse.

Reynolds stepped over the caution tape and, mesmerized by the sight of a sailboat resting on top of bilge blocks in the front part of the premises, proceeded as if in slow motion.

"Mike?" He heard the shrill voice again, its owner much closer this time.

"Traffic?" she said, taunting Reynolds about his late arrival.

"If only." He shook his head. "If only."

"Not even gonna ask," Heather replied.

He wouldn't tell even if she did.

"What do we have here?" Reynolds nodded in the direction of the bloodstained floor.

"You mean, what we did have here," Heather corrected. "Two bodies, the lab picked them up fifteen minutes ago. One here," she pointed toward the chalk outline closer to the exit, "a knife in the throat. Another over there," she pointed toward the stern of the boat, "shot through the head with a .45 hollow point, apparently by the first vic. Both have been dead for at least three hours now."

"Any chance the two did each other in?" Reynolds asked hopefully.

"Sorry, I've got no quick wrap-up for you just yet." Heather looked not in the least bit sorry. "And that's not merely my professional opinion speaking, which from what I hear you don't find too reliable, but also a mystery blood stain we found over by one of the bilge blocks."

"You're thinking that the blood might have belonged to the real knife-wielder?"

"It's a possibility we have to consider. Ballistics on the Kimber won't be ready until late afternoon, but as far as the knife goes, I can tell you now, they won't get anything off it."

"Why the hell not?" Reynolds asked.

"The handle is made out of unfinished wood," Heather said. "Even if the blood weren't so smudged, it would be near impossible to get a workable print off that surface."

"Damn," Reynolds swore. "Any witnesses?"

Heather shook her head. "Not that we know of. We're not

even sure how these guys got here; we found no cars outside."

"Is anybody checking on the taxis?"

"Not my field," Heather said. "Didn't you talk to Gomez on your way in?"

"I have yet to find the bastard," Reynolds grumbled.

"He said he'd be working with the tire tracks outside. Tom has found some deep ones next to the railroad car. Looks like someone tore out of there sometime recently."

"Could've been our knife thrower."

Heather shrugged her shoulders. "That's a possibility, but I wouldn't put too much hope into getting a good mold off those tracks. Not after half of the NYPD had parked out there earlier."

"Half of the NYPD?" Reynolds asked, confused. "Don't tell me one of the vics was the mayor."

"Nooo," Heather drawled, seemingly amused. "But we do have an ID on one of the bodies. Apparently there was a phone call prior to when these deaths occurred...."

CHAPTER II

Aya Morell holstered her weapon and stood motionless, anticipating approval.

"Nice shot, what can I say?" Gavin Wade leaned against the tinted glass wall that separated the gallery from the control booth beyond and watched her examine the carefully calculated damage to the target.

He couldn't help but notice the body hugging fit of her velvet jumpsuit, her flawless silhouette, as she drew the gun anew and weighed it in her hand lovingly.

"Kimber Custom II, 45 ACP, beveled side and rear serrations, match grade barrel and trigger group, polished breech face and full length guide rod. Accuracy and reliability." She spoke deliberately, with somewhat of a lack of intonation, as if reading from a manual.

Wade knew her to do that often, perhaps to counteract whatever emotion she wished to conceal.

What was it now? Sadness about leaving? Or relief? Gratitude for the gift? Discomfort for having to accept it? Or was she simply bored?

Two years of working alongside her and he still felt like an outsider, looking in without a key. Unable to read between the lines.

"I thought these were special order. How did you come by one?" Her attention remained consumed by the weapon.

"Don't ask, and you won't prove me a liar." Wade struggled to gain control of his voice. He never imagined it would be so hard to make his cues casual, to keep regret from seeping through. "Consider it a farewell present, something to remember me by."

A moment of hesitation, and she slid the gun back in the holster.

"Thank you, Gavin. Been a pleasure working with you."

"Level-headed as ever." He clicked his tongue, pushing the reminiscence aside. "And though she might look twenty-five, isn't she packing for an early retirement?"

"Packing for Arizona." Aya replaced the earmuffs to their designated spot, her voice regaining its color.

"Desert views?"

"And a job contract to follow."

"Well, nicely done, agent!" Wade rubbed his hands together theatrically. "What will it be then? A night watchman? A greengrocer? An exotic dancer?"

"That, my friend, is classified information." She smiled as she always did at the sense of her own superiority, and an awkward silence followed.

Was she truly superior? Was she the embodiment of perfection?

The closest he'd ever get, something whispered in Wade's ear as he made a final, desperate attempt to keep the growing ocean between them from icing over.

"Then the economists are right for once," he said with forced cheer, "one cannot live by pension funds alone." His humor fell short, unable to overcome the distance between them.

Something flickered within her eye; did he really see it?

Wade made a motion to seize her hand, then stopped abruptly.

Did she notice? Did she care?

"It's shame money, Gavin. You know that." Aya's voice was again hollow. "I'm not even sure I should let them buy me off."

Her last curt nod. Her footsteps heading out the door. The echo of her last good-bye, lingering behind.

CHAPTER III

The Mustang needed a new paint job and an engine overhaul, though Aya never seemed to have time to look for a better car. There were always things more important to do, places to be, people to meet. Her personal car was hardly an issue when she could hop into the government lease just as well.

But that was then.

Now, as Aya drove through the front gate of her destination point, she felt only relieved to have the endless journey behind her; thankful that the rear axle hadn't snapped from the weight of her expansive wardrobe; almost suffocated by the malfunctioning AC.

Was that all there was to feel? No regrets? No desire to turn back time? Undo what had been done? Avoid the uprooting of her whole life, her known universe?

Aya wasn't ashamed to admit that perhaps there was a slight taste of doubt in the jumble of her emotions, coated by a thick shell of determination. Who's perfect after all?

But what's done was done; there was no use in dwelling

about the past.

Dorothy was no longer in Kansas. She was in the land of deregulated plenty. A visitor, standing alone by the edge of a new world, a light breeze tossing her hair, an impregnable colossus of treated glass and black marble by the name of Neuetech towering before her.

She was here now, and hence exactly where she was supposed to be.

***

"On behalf of Neuetech, I'd like to welcome you to Phoenix." A man in Armani quickly covered the distance between the elevator door and the lounge. "Conrad Maltais, Chief of Security," he introduced himself with a smile and extended his arm for a handshake, his smooth tan and pearly white teeth nauseatingly wholesome.

Aya met his hand halfway, a giveaway army grip, hardly befitting the man's overall appearance of a suit salesman.

"Your reputation precedes you," he went on, barely awarding her another glance while they waited for the elevator to return.

Must be a new and ingenious way of testing new hires, Aya assumed. Assessing sensitivities by use of flattery and disregard combined. Unless she was drawing too much from his behavior, and the bastard was, in fact, simply too ignorant to know the truth about Aya's blemished career and too rude to bother looking her in the eye.

Either way, desensitized to intimidation from years of mingling in a testosterone-infused environment, Aya didn't hesitate to correct him. "You must mean my notoriety."

"That too." Maltais' lack of curiosity spoke for itself. "We consider it to be just a part of your expertise."

So he knew. Aya drew the obvious conclusion, that the man was not a narrow-minded cretin after all. Was that newsflash worthy of celebration?

The elevator door pinged open to reveal a mile-long corridor of metallic pastels and muted lights ahead. Her back still sticky with perspiration, Aya stepped out of the cab and followed Maltais' lead.

"How was your trip?" he inquired as if to disprove another of Aya's hopeful assumptions.

"Stifling." One word equally applied both to the weather and the drive itself.

"If you mean the heat, this summer's actually been pretty mild as far as local standards go. You'll get used to it after a while. Nothing a good night's sleep won't cure."

His step was light, like a cat's, while Aya's heel gave out a dull thud into the soft gray carpet.

"Your living arrangements have been taken care of," he continued. "You'll be staying in the 7th Street Marriott for the duration of the job, and if we do decide to take you on board as a permanent member of our staff, the company allows a certain grace period to help you find something more suitable. You're welcome to order anything you like off the menu free of charge, just another perk of working for the department. Call me personally if there's a problem at any point."

After what seemed like miles of walking, Maltais stopped at one of the indistinct gray doors, only identifiable by a number, and rummaged a key out of his pocket. "My office."

He invited her inside the modestly furnished suite, which was illuminated by a single fixture over the centerpiece desk.

"And here I have your badge, your cell phone, our standard issue Beretta 96 and handcuffs." He reached inside the desk drawer and laid out the listed items in a neat row.

"I will ask you to sign for receiving these. Should there arise a need for additional accessories, the cage will be happy to oblige. Now..." He opened and closed a filing cabinet. "...Before you plunge into an afternoon of leisure, I'd like you to get familiar with your primary assignment."

He took a seat at his desk and gestured Aya to the extra chair. She sat and waited patiently while he drew inspiration for his upcoming spiel from the file-folder before him.

"Commercial espionage proves to be a severe problem in a post-industrialized society," Maltais began, his eyes meeting Aya's at last. "Research and development has become a risky business."

"You're saying someone out there is tempted to risk it all for copy machine schematics?" Aya interrupted, wondering if the newly established direct approach signified the end of Maltais' mind games. She shuddered to think he might've actually found the test results beneficial.

"And more," Maltais affirmed. "Besides being one of the largest manufacturers of office equipment in the U.S., Neuetech has branches in pharmaceutics and experimental prosthetics. And we are not just talking about someone but about this particular individual..." he produced a photograph out of the file-folder and held it out for Aya to view, "...who has broken into our database to make off with a truckload of unpatented designs." He slid the rest of the file across the desk to her.

Aya leaned forward to collect the documents, the man in the photograph holding his perpetual smile. Early thirties, she would have guessed. Long sideburns and a few days without shaving were his only obstacles toward an otherwise perfect Polo moment. Ralph Lauren would approve.

"Why are you so sure he still has it?" Aya put the photograph back in the folder.

"We have our sources within the competing organizations, and they tell us those designs so far have not shown up."

"Then why don't you patent them now, before it's too late?"

Maltais sank back in his chair, his fingers crisscrossed in front of his chin, and spoke, as if he were explaining simple equations to a first-grader.

"Those projects were never meant to be put in production; they are rejects, flawed at the core."

Climate control whined on, taking over where Maltais' voice left off, and a stream of cold air slipped down Aya's damp shirt.

"If they are so useless, why worry about getting them back?" She shifted her chair to avoid the vent.

"We have our reasons," Maltais replied, all-knowing. "We have our ethics, whereas someone out there might not."

"Someone," Aya echoed. "What leads do we have on this special someone?"

"Not many." Maltais' tone was grim. "Our previous investigation turned out to be an outright flop, I'm ashamed to admit. A young, promising chemist, working at this facility, one day disappears after two years of impeccable service and leaves us with nothing to go by but traces of an outdated hacking program in his terminal. It's all in the file."

Aya flipped through the pages and fidgeted. Something

smelt fishy. "What makes you think I'll succeed where others failed?"

"You have a clear edge over your predecessors," Maltais answered matter-of-factly.

"And what might that be?"

"Your years of experience with the Bureau. And, besides," he got up to let her know the meeting was over, "you're a woman."

CHAPTER IV

"So, Wade, how did you survive Morell?" Wesley Shoener took his eye off the viewfinder and dropped a probing glance toward the driver's seat. "A 'delicate flower,' that one. Heard some wild stories going around."

A late night downpour had left the streets slick, the black asphalt dimly reflecting streetlights with its oil-like varnish. Gavin Wade watched the remaining drizzle spin cobwebs across the surface of the windshield and said nothing.

"What d'you two do in your spare time then?" The occupant of the passenger seat, however, preferred to cope with uneventful stakeouts by incessant taunting. "Did you play tennis? Share fashion tips? You were big-time buds, isn't that right?"

Wade suppressed an exasperated groan at the inevitable prospect of having to endure Shoener's conversation and concentrated on convincing himself that any such likelihood could be avoided by persistently ignoring him.

Not that Wade harbored any hard feelings towards the man. After all Shoener was just another one-track minded novice who treated silence as a shortfall in communication. One of those Darwinian varieties of form that, try as they might, never seem to rise above the level of irksome pests.

But despite such superficial make-up a man like Shoener must have been of some use. Perhaps, not there. Perhaps, not then. But somewhere, at some hypothetical point in time. Why else would the greater forces of natural selection grant the survival of a human gnat?

Why else, unless the entire concept of evolution was a myth, unless a daily trip to the gym and a three hundred dollar cell phone bill alone could account for purposeful existence?

"I wonder if one like that still reads historical romances." Not in the least bit put off by Wade's lack of interaction, Shoener drawled on, "I'd bet fifty bucks she does. Must be a real chore to hide that side of yourself...."

"Maybe you should go ahead and ask the AD for his opinion on the matter, when he wants to know why you didn't keep your eyes on the designated house. I'm sure he'd appreciate the graceful form of your thinly veiled insinuations." Before Wade could stop himself the words poured out of his mouth, and he was stunned to hear the intensity of anger that filled his voice.

Shoener blinked, equally taken aback, but his recovery was prompt, as he shrugged defensively. "You're a natural asshole, aren't you? I'm only trying to strike up a conversation."

"Then try talking about why we're sitting here, in this shithole of a town, in the middle of the night, orchestrating a local bust, when the cops in that van seem to be doing an equally useless job without our valuable contribution."

No other words were spoken. Shoener leaned toward the viewfinder of his camera, and Wade felt almost a prick of empathy toward the man's absent self-sufficiency.

Is that what it was? That knot in the bottom of Wade's stomach, that pent-up frustration? Is that what empathy felt like? Or was it that misplaced anger again, dressed in disguise? Anger at what exactly? Being stuck babysitting a malformed step on the evolutionary ladder? Losing the only friend he had to the martyrdom of federal bureaucracy? His own inability to corroborate Aya's line of defense, when she needed it most? All the injustices of the world combined?

Perhaps there was a lot more than Shoener's nagging that Wade had chosen to ignore at one time or another.

Perhaps, he was destined to sit in a stuffy rental all night long, staring down the dark facades of subsidiary housing, listening to the rain lash at the pavement with a newly acquired vigor, until he sorted out his values, his emotions....

"Someone's here." Shoener barged into Wade's thoughts with an urgent exhale and the whirring of electronic zoom.

But then again, abstract concepts of destiny and evolution could all be nothing but a load of horse manure, and it was time to stop theorizing and get back to the practical realities of life.

His reaction delayed, Wade grabbed the extra pair of binoculars off the dash and made a sweeping motion along the stretch of the road ahead. Great sinister elm trees, swaying in the wind. Rotted wood fences.

A black sedan flashing its brake lights at the far corner of the block. A man, clad in a long overcoat, exiting to go the rest of the way on foot.

"He's got the goods with him. He's heading for the house."

The shutter release clicked simultaneously with Shoener's uninvited commentary. "All that's left to do now is wait for an okay from our PD buddies over there."

In between the flutters of the windshield wipers Wade once again saw the house, dark and unwelcoming, its front door open to let the overcoat in.

And the silence reigned.

"Come on now." Wade heard Shoener's gun cock. "Let's do it and all go..."

Before Shoener could finish his plea, dull shots resonated from inside the house and through the night air.

After a slight delay, the back doors of the police van flew open with a pop, and a tactical squad spilt out into the street and sprinted toward the property.

"C'mon, that's as good as any sign." Shoener swung the car door open, the sticky humidity squalling into the cab.

"Hold it there." Wade's order cut Shoener's enthusiasm short. "We're not to make a move until a say-so."

Shoener, however reluctantly, shut the door and resorted to staring a hole through Wade's head rather than re-establishing the surveillance procedure.

"Eyes back on the target," Wade growled and brought his own binoculars closer to his face.

As he watched the TAC squad storm the entrance door of the house, Wade realized they were too late. He noticed a shadow separate from the darkness just outside the police line and move swiftly in the direction of the parked sedan. But not as swiftly as a running man would.

Wade adjusted his zoom,

"Shit, there's a hostage. The snitch has been compromised."

Whoever Fights Monsters

The man in the long overcoat hugged the informant with a gun at his victim's jaw. The living shield was dragged down the curb line toward the black sedan. The tactical team had been too slow to catch onto the existence of the hidden door on the side of the house and too late to cut off the suspect's exit route toward his car. Still shielded by his hostage, the man in the overcoat opened the sedan door just before pandemonium ensued.

Wade wasn't clear as to who fired first. Perhaps the suspect while trying to make a statement of contempt for the intelligence level of the police force. Perhaps, some trigger-happy rookie. By the time the black sedan sped off the scene, the TAC squad no longer held back. Their fire hit the getaway's taillights, bounced against the trunk, sparkled in the night over the informant's body, writhing in pain on the asphalt.

The informant's screams drowned by the downpour, Wade punched the gearshift and stepped on the gas, Shoener's 'get me in firing distance' ringing in his ear.

In an attempt to make up for the suspect's head start, Wade cut through someone's lawn and into a narrow alley. Knocking down a few garbage cans on the way, he emerged on the other end of the block, the car sliding on the rain-slicked road as he braked for a sharp turn ahead.

Shoener rolled down the passenger side window in anticipation of his chance for a shot, while Wade floored the gas pedal.

Streets unraveled in a quick succession of flashing red lights, speed bumps and unexpected turns. The black sedan, only a few houses ahead now, was not about to lose more ground. Just as Shoener made his first go at the suspect's tires, the getaway driver swerved, almost clipping a semi parked by the curb, and drove into the back parking lot of a small strip shopping mall.

Wade stayed on course, hoping to intercept the sedan as it circled the building, but instead of pulling back onto the street, the sedan rammed the flimsy guardrail and flew over the shallow ditch beyond.

Wade didn't dare to follow. He sped down the empty street, until he could make a hard left turn. Once again he found himself directly behind the suspect's car. The black sedan was slowly losing ground.

Shoener aimed and fired. And fired again. One, two, three, in rhythmic intervals. That was the last thing Wade remembered before the getaway car spun out dead ahead of them.

CHAPTER V

There comes a point in every young woman's life when a question arises as to whether comfort should prevail over style.

Dressing up, dressing down; all the hidden attributes and connotations that go with attire.

Should we use clothes to express who we are? Should they disguise our real self instead? Does dressing like a slut actually entail being one?

Aya Morell was no Erin Brokovich, though her elevated levels of interest toward form-fitting apparel were undeniable. The way she viewed it, everything hinged on the matter of balance, on choosing the best of both worlds. One wouldn't want to be caught chasing down a fugitive in stilettos, but, come on, how often did she actually use her physical talents? A typical course of an official investigation rather preferred to root itself in the sinkhole of circumstantial evidence, paper-pushing tedium, rules and limitations, the very things that clashed with Aya's independent nature.

Perhaps her interest in clothing had once begun as a

diversion, an obstinate attempt to hold on to her individuality. Though eventually the fashion freak inside her had settled into an inseparable part of who she was.

Whoever designed Phoenix's 7th Street Marriott must have ascribed to a similar view on escapism. Aya couldn't help noticing the adjoining mini shopping mall, as she walked through the hotel lobby toward the reception desk. She gazed longingly down the length of the glass umbilical at a Charlotte Rousse outlet, but in the end refrained from satisfying the urge. Matters more pressing than maxing out her credit cards were at hand.

Like waiting for the concierge to get her key, like getting the unpacking process over with, like settling into her room, her new home away from the home she'd never had. Studying the files, plunging into the case.

But first....

***

Aya tested the water and drew the curtain. She let the shower run while she pulled off her jeans and musty T-shirt to leave them lying in a pile on the flawless clean of the bathroom tile.

She placed the Beretta on a shelf over the stall, unstrapped the gun belt and stepped into the mist of steam. Warm water forgivingly streamed through her short, sun-bleached hair, styling gel melting away, taking her anxiety with it. A river, running down her stomach, circling patterns into the drain.

She thought of her old apartment, with its all too familiar creature comforts, but only for a second. And then no more.

The memory remained just that. Another fuzzy aspect of the bygone era, another lost cause, a purposeless undertaking to be written off. And the generic hotel room in which she had found herself suddenly felt like the only thing ever real.

Foggy mirror restored to clarity, Aya wrapped a soft towel around her middle and, positively refreshed, entered the bedroom.

She pulled her long legs up on the powder blue of the bed covers, set the gun on the pillow beside her, and opened the case file Maltais had given her.

Ryuiji Oishi, she read the first and only name on the suspect list. Born in Osaka. Age four, family moves to the States. Age fourteen, parents die in a motor vehicle accident. Age nineteen, following his father's legacy, he enters Princeton to obtain a degree in chemical engineering. Postgraduate research in non-Newtonian fluid mechanics. Recommended for a job opening at Neuetech by a Dr. Gail Hager, the since retired head of the synthetics department. Contact sheets, as well as a jewel case containing the CD with the visual surveillance recording of the crime in progress, were attached.

Aya went through the evidence at one gulp and felt her head beginning to spin. She realized she was incredibly hungry. Starving. Her earlier decision to skip a proper breakfast in favor of decreasing her travel time came back to haunt her with a migraine.

She grabbed the phone and dialed Room Service to order a bit of Chinese food and a whole lot of over the counter analgesics.

One hand keeping the towel from slipping straight down to her ankles, the other never letting go of the her gun, Aya fumbled with the door knob and watched the look of perplexed curiosity on the bellboy's face turn into a horrified grimace, as she ushered him in with a sweep of the barrel.

CHAPTER VI

Wade awoke with the taste of blood on his lips and a stinging pain in his eye. With a hiss, the steam escaped from the cracked radiator. He lifted his head off of the steering wheel, the view through the windshield blocked by the crumpled hood. Shoener slumped, unconscious, in the passenger seat, his blood-smeared face looking upward, his sluggish hand still clutching his Glock.

Wade unclipped his seatbelt and reached for the radio only to find it smashed against the mangled dashboard. He swept the trickling blood off his eyelid and pushed the already ajar, misaligned car door open the rest of the way.

At first there was nothing but the numbness of confusion. Realization followed with a wave of searing pain. With someone's strung out voice ahead.

"There's been an accident.... The corner of 4th and Hickory.... At least one person is dead for sure...." A man stood drenched by a sideswiped Continental, screaming into his cell phone. "I think

I'm okay." His face was turned away from Wade, transfixed by something in front of the suspect's car.

Dazed, Wade walked forward toward the dark intersection.

One more step, another wind gust, before he could see as well.

The force of the impact had thrown the black sedan they'd been chasing onto the sidewalk. An electric pole just ahead leaned to one side, its dead cables strewn over the car's hood and the pavement around. The getaway driver's body lodged in the broken windshield, a glint of lightning pitchfork in his frozen stare.

CHAPTER VII

Heat was a nuisance. Swearing that she should have taken a cab, Aya left the Mustang roasting in the driveway and walked up the ramp, toward the front door of the house.

And a squat little house it was, bland as it could be. Plain vinyl siding and a tar roof. Hardly an obvious source of pride for its renowned owner.

Aya shrugged, her curiosity stirred, but not so that it showed, and rang the bell. She then stepped back, tugged down on her shorts to keep the gun strap out of view, and waited.

"A beautiful young lady at my doorstep." Gray hair presented itself at the level of her waist, and Aya looked down at the man and his wheelchair. "To what do I owe such pleasure?"

"Dr. Hager?" She made a quick motion forward, an attempt to conceal her start at the sight of a beard that had boldly gone where no man in his right mind would allow it to go. Not unless he were auditioning for the part of Merlin the magician.

"Yes, Gail Hager, PhD. That would be me," the Merlin wannabe confirmed, his wheelchair revving, his mouth disputably shaping into a smile behind the thick beard. "How can

33

I make that worry leave your angelic face?"

"A two hundred thousand dollar donation to the Aya Morell retirement fund would go a long way." She shook the old man's hand.

His palms felt moist and sticky. It could almost make a non-believer break down and order a year's supply of skin sanitizer. Aya wondered if it wasn't a new sales gimmick invented by Purell and if Hager wasn't their top agent in medieval disguise.

"Feisty," Hager hummed, eyeing her down. Or rather up, considering the vantage point. "I like that." He let go of her hand and turned the wheelchair around. "Come on in, make yourself at home. You look hot, would you like something cool to drink?"

"Yes, thank you." Aya wiped her fingers against the back of her shorts and stepped out of the brutal sun. The door slammed shut behind her.

The interior of Hager's house was a dramatic contrast to its uninspired facade.

The large living room looked like a pioneer cabin, with walls decoupaged to look like logs, hardwood floors prettified by a bear rug and a multitude of partial carcasses of wildlife, mounted in all the unlikely places. A photograph of Hager's younger self proudly displaying a rifle and a dead duck hung above the fireplace.

Gruesome, Aya thought, shuffling her foot through a pile of yellow paperbacks beside the coffee table. Yet curious.

"There you are." The old man reappeared to hand her a glass of lemonade, while saving one for himself. "Sit down, why don't you?"

She did, trying hard to avoid the wolf jaws sprawled across the armrest of the love seat.

"Do you read L'Amour?" Hager asked.

Aya failed to mask her expression of literary ignorance.

"Great literature. Simpler times. When men were men and sheep were nervous," he giggled, apparently convinced of the irresistible qualities of his humor.

Aya turned away to roll her eyes.

"Well now, you still haven't told me what brings you to my humble abode." He set his drink aside and crisscrossed his fingers in anticipation.

Aya started on her well-thought-out lie. "I'm writing an article as a part of journalism certificate program at Phoenix College."

"An article about me?" Hager didn't let her finish. "How absolutely wonderful. I won't say no, if you're worried about that. Makes an old man feel like a real celebrity." He giggled again. "Come on then; break out your note book. Let's give it a go. What would you like to know first?"

Aya was slightly taken aback by Hager's eagerness, but hardly disappointed by not having to share the remainder of her cover story.

"Tell me about your line of specialty," Aya began, taking a taste of her lemonade. She puckered up at the lack of sugar and summoned all her will power in order not to spit all over the wolf jaws.

"I hold a degree in molecular biology and a career in pharmaceutics, both of which found an application in my ground-breaking written works. Apparently that's what it takes for a bit of fame," Hager chuckled, the tip of his beard unavoidably colliding with his protruding belly. "I enjoy staying in the loop, giving lectures, grading papers. Semi-retirement as a part-time academic has its small perks. Visits like these...."

Aya offered a statement rather than a question. "You're no longer with Neuetech."

"No." A slight shadow came over Hager's countenance. "That's all done and buried. We've had a minor difference of opinion a short while ago, but all that proved to be of no significance."

"Why do you say that?" she asked.

Hager pointed at his wheelchair.

"Who might you think is paying for this? And doctor's bills. And physical therapy."

Although tormented by thirst, Aya dared not attempt another swallow of the lemonade.

"What was the nature of your conflict with Neuetech?" she asked.

Hager took in a good mouthful of liquid before deciding on an answer. "I've always been an avid believer in the future of Neuetech's vision, but sometimes I would find their methods," he paused, hesitant, "dubious."

"Unethical?" Aya suggested.

"Now watch your tongue, young lady," Hager's bushy eyebrows flew upward. "That's a harsh word you're using, and I never said anything like that." As his eyes slid beneath Aya's face to look at her breasts, his momentary rage dispersed. "Why don't you ask me about my early breakthroughs instead?"

For a moment Aya considered going by the book, sticking to her cover, with caution as the first rule, but the mere thought of exposure to hours of chauvinistic pompousness awakened that part of her that always chose a shortcut.

Besides, collapsing from dehydration remained an imminent

threat.

"Were they anything like those of Ryuiji Oishi?" Aya went straight to the point.

"Oh yes," Hager replied, her purpose still beyond him. "Ryuiji, he had that magnificence akin to his beloved sitar player. A bright young star, not unlike myself at that age. He turned to me as his mentor and shared his beautiful dream of making the world a better place with the things he could achieve by working for Neuetech." For a second Hager seemed lost in reverie.

Aya didn't quite grasp the reference to a sitar player, but to each his own. She decided to ignore it and stick to the topic.

"Things like lifting company's data?" she asked.

For a moment Hager simply stared, his fall to reality too abrupt for his aging brain to catch up. Then he spoke. "What are you talking about?" A mere whisper.

Aya saw his jaw quiver. "I'm asking if you were a party, whether by knowledge or action, to Oishi's plan to rob Neuetech of its intellectual property." Aya's voice was metronome-like. "And whether you're aiding him now by concealing his whereabouts."

"You're not a college student, are you?" Hager's face drained of color, his fingers gripped tight around his glass. "You work for *them*! They sent you here trying to get to me. Bastard low lives!" Without a warning the glass left his grip and flew in Aya's direction across the room, its shattering shriek blending into the old man's roar. "I've already done everything you people asked of me!"

What should have been a jolt of panic felt strangely like relief, Aya was surprised to realize as she jumped off the love seat and out of harm's way. Almost as if she found Hager's untamed nature refreshingly sincere.

"I know nothing else. Tell them that! Go and tell them that!"

She backed away into the hallway, "Your cooperation or not, it won't take long to get to the bottom of the matter."

"No such animal." His speech was suddenly composed. "The bottom is a bottomless pit. Now go."

CHAPTER VIII

The office welcomed Wade with its familiar angularity. The heavy oak writing desk, put together with traditional mid-western quality, sturdy brass trimmings of the matching set of chairs and cabinets, everything their owner would refer to as 'the real thing.' Perfect for an omnipresent, omniscient being of quick temper.

The man at the desk was, however, far from perfection. The thick layer of paperwork that littered the cabinet tops and the floor in the back of the office (a cleaning woman's nightmare that quickly earned a convenient acronym and was strategically referred to by the employees as a Continual Repository Advancement Process), as well as the man's outrageously shaped sand-colored moustache, an ungodly sight in its own right, testified as to the truth of his imperfection. The man had been recently divorced, though no one besides the staff psychologist was to address the fact, not even under the most dire of circumstances.

"What's this?" The man at the desk glanced at the sheet of

39

paper that had landed in front of him and smoothed out his moustache.

That familiar, unempathetic voice made Wade uneasy. "My letter of resignation, sir."

Assistant Director Tieri studied the sheet more carefully, his eyes, a washed-out color of bewilderment, shifting back and forth across the page. "A change in personal values?" he quoted. "You gotta be kidding! What in the world... Now?" Tieri seemed struck speechless. A clear sign, Wade was well aware, of an impending sensory overload.

Wade was ready. "I blew the Christensen case," his hand involuntarily reached toward the adhesive bandage on his still aching temple, "which makes my competence questionable."

"You blew... What're you babbling about?" Tieri fumed, as he let go of the letter. But the ephemeral floodgate that separated Tieri's notorious supply of raw verbal sewage from the civilized world outside held. "The case wasn't yours to blow. Locals claimed jurisdiction, we gave it to them, they weren't even grateful enough to let us in on all the details. They fucked up their snitch's cover, almost fried the guy with their wire and then got him shot by opening fire in hostage situation." He exhaled his frustrations. "I could go on, you know, but nothing on the blunder reel would include your actions. You stopped the contact from getting away with the money which was, if anything, the only positive outcome of the entire operation."

"I stopped him by causing his death and endangering my own partner's life." Wade did his best to give the statement a composed air, although composure couldn't be further from his state of mind.

"But you did stop him." As if responding to Wade's effort,

Tieri's voice dropped an octave. Or could it be those late hours in Dr. Danes' office paying off at long last?

A moment of silence was followed by Wade's quiet retort. "How do my actions differ from those of Agent Morell's?"

"Not that Morell business again!" Tieri put a hand to his forehead. "Tell me you aren't pining for her, Wade."

"She did what she had to do to stop a criminal from getting away." Wade ignored the personal remark.

"She shot a man in cold blood!" Forgetting all his hours in counseling, Tieri contained his frustration no longer. "Agent Morell overstepped her call. She thought rules didn't apply to her, she thought she was above the law. Yet she's only an instrument of it, as much as any of us here. We're team players, Wade. An individualist like her does not have a place at the Bureau."

Flustered, Tieri held his hand up to his mouth, as if to take a silent vow. For a brief moment, Wade was under the impression the Assistant Director would never speak again. Tieri did, however, although with a much steadier tone, the floodgate forced back in place.

"I see now, I underestimated her influence on you. I believed I was doing everyone a favor by giving you a rookie partner as a challenge. I thought it would help your concentration, but I was wrong. Now you're barely thirty and ready to throw your whole life away on a whim" He shook off his exasperation to collect a strained smile. "I remember your first day at the office. Fresh out of the Academy. Sure of yourself, not to mention full of it. A young man, gifted with the power of raw determination and an honest heart that would guide it. A real go-getter. Then along came Morell, and look at you now. Defeated. She's nothing but a destructive force, don't you see?"

Another pause followed, Wade clenched his fingers behind his back, struggling to clear his mind before Tieri's words had a chance to sink in.

The Assistant Director made a sudden change of subject "What would you say to a couple of weeks in New York? Take off, see the city, catch some Broadway. A nice three-star hotel to stay in. No new partners to worry about. What d'you say?"

"I doubt I can afford a three-star hotel," Wade muttered.

"All paid for by a friend of mine, who was blessed by inheriting one. Along with a housing complex in Newark and some dozen apartment buildings all over the state." Tieri sniffed to express a mild level of contempt.

"I expect I'd be left in your friend's debt?"

"A favor easily returned by clearing up another of his paranoid delusions." Tieri, now fully recovered from his earlier relapse, gestured to Wade to sit down. "Ever since receiving his inheritance six years ago, he has believed everyone is out to get him. His personal assistant lies; his banker is ripping him off; the milkman is trying to poison him. Now he's convinced that someone is blackmailing him."

"Nevertheless, he trusts your opinion?" Wade threw one leg over the other and leaned against the hard back of the office chair. He remembered all too well that feeling of safety he could only achieve while immersed in his work. Knowing a case, predicting its outcome, was as close to seeing the future as one would ever get. A chance to come to terms with one's fate before it arrived. And as he felt himself slowly succumb to that eternal longing for closure, Wade was no longer sure he could leave the Bureau.

"His father. Best friend I ever had." Tieri's fingers drummed against the desk. "Besides, I'm too far away to pose an immediate threat. Another reason he won't report any of it to the police, they tend to meddle a bit too much for his taste. And besides, on a bad day he thinks they're after him as well."

"So what is this blackmail business?" Wade allowed himself to ask.

"That, unfortunately, he won't discuss over the phone. But I'm sure it'll turn out to be nothing, just as any other time before. I'd go if I were you. I'd go myself if I could take off right now. You'll have fun. Looks to me like you could use some. And afterwards, do what you will. Go ahead and quit. I'm not gonna stop you. That is if you still wish to." Tieri picked Wade's letter back up off the desk. "What d'you say we file this away for now?"

Wade got up before giving an answer. "I'll have to get back to you on that one," he said, and in that second of hesitation he knew he had lost. He realized it just as surely as Tieri knew the perfect opportunity to assume a patronizing stance.

"I'll be expecting you to decide by tomorrow morning...and Gavin," Wade endured the last of Tieri's meaningful pauses, "I told him you were the best I've got."

CHAPTER IX

"You went to see who?" The stout, increasingly hyper inhabitant of Neuetech's IT Solutions burst out laughing. "Gail, the crazy pedophile?"

Instead of going straight to Oishi's former workstation, Ronnie Halprin (for that, if one were to trust the accuracy of ID badges, appeared to be the man's name) preferred to give Aya a roundabout introduction to IBM craftsmanship. Along with one on the inner workings of the eighteenth century whaling vessels and his very own hopes of restoring his receding hairline. All apparently equally important on Ronnie's scale of priorities.

"Gail?" Some fifteen, twenty minutes later his soliloquy had gone full circle. "Gail doesn't talk to people, let alone allow them inside his house."

"You know him well?" Aya inquired, relieved to be once more blissfully unconcerned with the top ten commercial uses of Narwhal blubber.

"Let's say well enough to keep my kids away from the creep," Ronnie replied, proceeding with the further display of his constant, tugging need to over-explain. "That is if I had any kids. He eats pretty young'uns for breakfast. Girls, boys, he won't care. I'm sure that's the reason Oishi got hired so easily. I'm sure that's the reason you got to see Gail's living room. D'you know how he got that wheelchair?"

Aya waited for him to elaborate, not exactly holding her breath in anticipation.

"Groped some little intern. Her punk-ass boyfriend got pissed, shot him in the back, pow!" Ronnie's finger pulled an invisible trigger. "Paralyzed. Administration went to a lot of trouble to hush that up. That's when he got bumped into retirement. Like that would stop the perv. Teaching at some community college now. A menace to morality."

Ronnie talked away the entire stretch of the main ChD level corridor, only suspending his 'engaging' narrative long enough to enable Aya's occasional effort at steering the conversation.

"What about Oishi; did he seem trustworthy?"

"He was a good kid." Ronnie buttoned up his lab coat and faced a pair of glass doors at the end of the hallway. "We had an occasional beer together. Promising new talent, all that. Must've been some precious stuff to turn him so."

"You don't believe he planned it from the start?" Aya watched him hastily input an access code.

"Oishi, a hard-core spy?" Ronnie walked inside a mid-size chamber, glass sliding out of the way. "A couple of months ago I would've sworn the thought was preposterous. But now... Hell, I don't know."

***

The Chemical Analysis and Development Lab was one of many adjoining airtight compartments that comprised the bulk of ChD level. Its intense fluorescence disoriented Aya for a moment.

White Formica counter tops littered with myriads of test tubes and petri dishes; chrome coated wash basins; microscopes and monitors lashed out at Aya's unprepared eye as the motion sensors brought the lab facilities on line.

Momentarily blinded, Aya halted at the threshold before she

could continue on into the inhospitable, shadowless chaos.

"Here you go." Ronnie circled the perimeter of the desktop machinery and stood beside a select monitor. "The undisturbed crime scene."

He never failed to make a pompous declaration.

Aya followed in Ronnie's footsteps toward the median. Her eyes gradually acclimating to the harsh light, she studied Oishi's workstation from the top down. A company screen saver, an orderly arrangement of pencils and blank notebooks, a drawer full of scissors, labels and mending supplies. Aya slid her fingers across the back of the keyboard, compulsively checking for signs of dust.

"Was he always this tidy?"

"Pretty much," Ronnie nodded, thus producing his shortest answer yet.

"No picture frames, no personal objects," Aya commented. "Do you recall him ever having any?"

"I can't say I do, no." Ronnie leaned on the hard drive box, as if to rest. Had he finally talked himself into exhaustion? One could only hope.

"You mentioned the two of you having a drink. Was there anything in particular you talked about?" she asked.

"Ponies, mostly," Ronnie knitted his brow in concentration.

"Was he a betting man?" Aya sat down in a swivel chair and tapped the mouse to unveil a password prompt.

"You better believe it," Ronnie chuckled. "Couldn't wait till Sunday morning to take off for Turf Paradise."

"Gambling debts?" Aya asked.

"He usually got lucky, from what he'd tell you. He even said he'd saved enough to buy a horse of his own with his winnings.

A yearling. Wanted to train it himself and everything."

"And did he? Did he buy one?"

"I suppose he did," Ronnie shrugged. "Yes, I believe he did."

"Do you know where he kept it?" Aya asked, glad to finally find a subject worthy of a follow-up.

"No, not really." Ronnie shook his head. "He mentioned renting a place somewhere, but he wasn't specific."

"Can you tell me anything else about this horse? Its name? The seller's name? The date of purchase? Anything?" Aya persisted.

Ronnie exhaled. "You have to understand, I wasn't as much into all the technical specs of horse racing as Oishi. I only put my money on a sure thing once in a blue moon, no more."

Oishi's horse was definitely a thing to look into. Too bad Ronnie didn't know more. Aya made it her firm intent to drive over to the track first thing the next morning and see what she could dig up.

"Turf Paradise, huh?" she voiced her thought and leaned back in her chair.

"A place where dreams are made and broken," Ronnie said with added pathos.

"And talking about breaking," Aya segued back to the matter of computer hacking. "How hard is it, generally speaking, to break though the security measures on this particular terminal?"

"For someone from the inside?" Ronnie specified. "Someone who's got the right idea how to go about it?"

"Meaning?" Aya scrutinized Ronnie's shifty eyes.

"We've run a couple of surface scans. The word is Splinter."

Ronnie's announcement left Aya's expression blank. He shook his head again, impatiently, at the prospect of supplying an explanation. "Have you ever seen a state of the art dinosaur trap in your lifetime?"

"I couldn't say I have." In the light of Ronnie's prior verbal exercises on whaling, Aya had her doubts on whether the ancient reptiles had anything to do with the current situation.

"Right," Ronnie proceeded, regaining his exuberance. "There's no need to make a trap now; dinosaurs have been extinct for millions of years. The Splinter virus is that dinosaur. A has been. I personally haven't heard from it in good ten years. Most people would consider an active shield that concentrates on the likes of Splinter outdated." He lifted his eyebrows consequentially. Not that Aya grasped such consequences to their full extent.

"And how would one get his hands on a virus like that?"

"Well, technically speaking..." Ronnie couldn't resist the opportunity to show-off. "It's not even a virus. It's a Trojan, modified to attack specific parameters. Meaning, though it's malicious, it has no way of replicating automatically. But where someone could get it, that's a tough one. The original version, I'd say collectors. Modified, the black market. I'd be lying if I said I knew for sure." Ronnie shrugged before adding a 'by the way.' "I love the way you talk. This sort of detachment about your voice, very interesting."

Aya's eyes were still staring at the password request when Ronnie's peculiar compliment turned into a question.

"Don't get much excitement in your line of work, do you?" he asked.

"Not lately." She pushed off with her legs, away from the terminal. The swivel chair rolled noisily across the tile floor, as she got up.

CHAPTER X

Wade turned over and opened his eyes to a mute stream of TV images. For a minute disoriented, paralyzed by the gravitational pull, he blankly stared at the screen, Tieri's farewell still ringing in his ear.

Vanna White pranced across the stage to reveal a letter, her stance triumphant, as she paused to contemplate the finished phrase.

"You're the best I've got." Were Tieri's words aimed to inspire him? Was that what he thought Wade needed to regain, inspiration? Was that how disenchantment appeared to an unsuspecting bystander? A simple incident of lacking inspiration; how hard could that be to fix? Throw in a couple of perks, a little paid vacation and, as with a case of minor nerve damage, the feeling would bounce back soon enough.

A Cadillac commercial flashed onto the TV screen. Wade's mind began its ascent toward full consciousness, toward 'here and now', the leaden weight of atmospheric pressure releasing its hold on his body.

He lifted his arm off the mattress and looked at his watch.

Six forty-two? Good god. He must have slept for at least three hours, an unavoidable effect, personal experience had proven, of air travel.

He found his gun and his wallet safely stashed under his pillow, his usual ritual when sleeping in unfamiliar places, yet he had no recollection of his intention to doze off.

Shit, the phone call! The thought made him jump out of bed. He had missed the phone call!

Knocked off balance by the false feeling of weightlessness, Wade almost tripped over the corner of his suitcase sticking out from under the bed as he stumbled back to the nightstand.

No, no messages. He double checked the user-friendly display window of the answering machine and, still dissatisfied, grabbed his room key and headed down to the lobby.

***

Loria Inn, a glorious creation, or rather a creature in its own right, a gilded slumbering dragon, had watched the century fly by with proud disregard. It saw seasons change, fashions falter as its many masters flourished and went down to their graves. The pampered dragon, trapped, but not tamed, listened to the shadows of whispers, pondered, searching for its chance to break free of the marble shell. Its heart, the great ivory hall, waited to beat again.

"No, sir.... Yes, sir.... I'm well aware of the fact that you're only staying here for the night, but..." The somewhat unnerved voice of the concierge resonated within the vertiginous walls of the hall. "Sir, that is not something our policy permits."

Curious about the nature of the unfolding conflict, Wade moved closer to the check-in desk only to witness the man at the front of the line storm off in frustration.

"Tough case?" Wade inquired, his idle curiosity wishing the concierge would dwell on his difficult customer.

But the star of the lobby already had his professional face back on, his expression impenetrable. "How may I be of assistance, sir?"

Wade cleared his throat to assume an equally grave tone. "I was wondering if the answering machine in my room was in proper working order," Wade began, then hastily tacked his room number to the end of the sentence, as he noticed the concierge reach for the hotel logbook. "I had a three o'clock meeting with Mr. Loria. Someone was supposed to call and let me know when he was ready to see me. I must've missed..."

The concierge didn't let him finish." Oh yes, Mr. Loria is in a session at the moment."

"Excuse me?" Wade, as any customer in his position, was clearly in need of a further explanation.

"He's with his therapist," the concierge added reluctantly. "Quite unscheduled."

"Any ideas on when they might be finished?"

"I'm afraid I don't have that information, sir."

The concierge's robotic demeanor was becoming increasingly annoying. More than ever Wade wished he knew the secret to his predecessor's success at making the automaton lose his cool.

"Was anyone planning on notifying me?" Wade's voice gave away his irritation.

The concierge remained not in the least bit rattled. "Of course, sir. We will let you know as soon as Mr. Loria's ready for you. Anything else I can do for you, sir?"

"No," Wade answered curtly and started to walk away, only to turn back around a moment later. "On second thought, there is," he said, Tieri's recipe for treating insufficient inspiration coming back to him with a reminder. "Which way is the bar?"

CHAPTER XI

The hotel suite proved to be as austere as Oishi's workstation.

There were no personal touches apparent in the tidy arrangements of stationary, the neat stacks of JoC weekly, the minimal selection of bath products and bland clothing.

There was nothing out of the ordinary in the medicine cabinet and the desk drawers. Empty.

Suddenly overpowered, stifled by the hounding eye of the weathered hotel clerk, Aya stepped out on the balcony.

She leaned over the railing for no particular reason, except, perhaps, to establish the whereabouts of her own room, and felt the light breeze ruffle her hair.

Aya couldn't decide on how to treat Oishi's unequivocally Spartan habits. Should she think of them simply as the man's little compulsions, quirks? Or were they his way of hiding something? A way of being prepared for flight at any given time? A proof of his guilt?

"Pretty good distance there, if one's looking for a jump..."

Like a shadow, a scrawny old crone of a hotel clerk materialized at Aya's side, mumbling at the quiet street below. "So is Mr. Oishi in some kind of trouble?" that raspy, filled to the brim with melancholy voice asked. "He's not, is he?"

"No, no trouble," Aya lied and changed the subject to discourage further questions. "You've been working here a while, haven't you?" She walked back inside, knowing the clerk would follow.

"Fourteen years, rain or shine." The clerk stopped at the threshold, toying with a key chain.

"How well did you get to know Mr. Oishi? He stayed here a while, didn't he?"

"Two years in all. But no, I didn't know him that well." The clerk took a beat to add a meaningful 'obviously.' "He seemed very private. Extremely mild-mannered. Charming."

That little gem of a description did not do much to help the case along, Aya thought and tried approaching the inquiry from a different angle. "Did he get any visitors? Any personal correspondence you happen to remember? Long distance calls?"

The clerk shook her head despondently.

"How many guests do you have staying here now?" Aya paced the floor, ready to move on to more productive pastures as the current conversation seemed to be heading nowhere. "Ones whose rooms are being paid for by Neuetech?"

"I could get you a list if you like." The clerk's wrinkled mouth produced the first halfway helpful answer so far. "I could ask the manager to pull up the records when he gets in."

"Please do. And while you're at it, go ahead and check as far back as the stored data goes. Your assistance would be indispensable." Aya's nervous footsteps assumed a sense of direction as they veered toward the exit door. "And before I go, one last question. Is it common practice for Neuetech employees to live out of a hotel room for two full years?"

Aya dropped a final glance over her shoulder, expecting the clerk to answer, but all she received was another heartsick shake of the head.

CHAPTER XII

The colonial outpost of Turf Paradise, with its 1400 acres of what used to be barren desert, lay a mere twenty-five miles from the heart of the burgeoning metropolis.

The combined effort of light Sunday traffic, absent police speed traps, and an eighty-five miles per hour breeze provided somewhat of a relief from the merciless heat of the roasting concrete until Aya pulled off onto the service ramp.

Disregarding a red light and the line of cars behind it, Aya ran over a curb and pulled into the parking lot.

She drove around in search of a shady spot and, finding none vacant, pulled up next to a Porsche. She left her windows down, as a future affirmation to her stern belief in the inability of criminal element to appreciate a metal hodge-podge of peeling paint, compared to a sleek body of fine Italian craftsmanship.

"Hey, old mare," Aya patted the discolored roof of her seasoned Mustang. "Can you sense your kin yet?" She slammed the heavy door shut.

"And again, this beautiful Sunday afternoon, ladies and

gentlemen, welcome to Turf Paradise!"

The coke dispenser swallowed another quarter and spit out a can of diet soda, as the amplified announcement boomed across the stands.

"It is eleven o'clock sharp and there you have it, a 1&1/17 mile handicap with a purse of $24,000, and if you haven't bet on Jay Black yet, you've just missed that two minute warning."

Aya sifted through the crowd before proceeding toward the betting booth.

"A relative newcomer, an undisputed champion at his home Aqueduct, Jay Black is a magnificent three-year thoroughbred colt owned by John Melbourne."

Instead of directly approaching a teller, she delayed, perplexed by the variety of scores running across the totalisator screen.

"And we have a definite front-runner; quickly, but to no surprise, Jay Black seizes the lead."

"Ma'am, are you in need of assistance?" The teller acknowledged her confusion, and Aya made her advance.

"A penny for your memories." She leaned on the window ledge to pass a photograph.

"Wasn't it too early to become overconfident? Signal Tower, a five-year old speed horse, suddenly slips up to second position and proceeds to crowd Jay Black back down to the rail."

"This man, do you see him here often?" Aya asked.

The teller held the photograph close to his glasses. "I can't say I ever have seen him at all," he finally pronounced.

"At the top of the stretch Jay Black falters. Signal Tower pounces, followed by Morning Tune sprinting through the remaining hole. Off he goes, and Morning Tune, I can't believe it,

Morning Tune stealing a two-length advantage!"

"You sure?" Aya pressed. "His name is Ryuiji Oishi. He might've been one of the horse owners."

The teller shrugged and returned the photograph without explanation.

"What a letdown, Jay Black finally gives way and bears out unable to keep up. No one can blame the boggy soil here."

The maintenance workers she stopped were equally unsuccessful at recognizing the man in the photograph, in spite of Aya's best effort at engaging her Spanish language skills.

"And we have Signal Tower and Morning Tune side by side coming into the final stretch. Neither seems to be gaining, but wait, Signal Tower charges ahead. Did you just see that? Signal Tower wins by a nose! There you have it!"

**

The announcer's commentary trailing off, Aya turned away from the window and pulled up a stool in the half-empty Silks Room Bar.

"Nice weather like this, who wants to be stuck inside?" The bartender's observation was unsolicited, and Aya struggled to repress a negative rejoinder. Without raising her eyes off the photograph, she ordered a drink and was left to silently enjoy her day's worth of air-conditioning.

The snapshot had been taken outside. Oishi stood against fuzzy green blotches of the background, his unruly black hair disheveled by the wind, his dark eyes squinting at the sunlight even more than a grin would require.

"What is it you're thinking of?" Aya whispered, tracing the

outline of his thin nose and narrow cheekbones with the tip of her finger.

"Your Perrier with lemon, madam." The bartender reappeared, along with a tall glass and a stack of assorted coasters. "Someone you know?" He nodded at the picture.

"Someone I wish I knew better." Aya scrutinized the bartender. Blond, blue-eyed. Your standard issue toy-boy, she thought dismissively.

"A blind date?" The bartender ran his hand through the waves of his hair in a clear act of vanity.

"Blind is the word." Aya pulled the wrapper off a straw.

"May I?" The bartender reached for the photograph before Aya could offer it to him.

His pupils bore into the image. Aya watched him pensively rub his forehead and, then light up with recognition.

"The guy who owns Sitar Player, right?" He hit the picture against his knuckles.

Sitar Player, so that's what Oishi's horse was called. For some reason the name sounded more familiar to Aya's ears than it should have. Aya didn't care for horses enough to even think about keeping up with the current racing events. And she was fairly positive she hadn't come across that particular word combination anywhere else lately. Not unless she had heard someone else speak the name before, at a time when it seemed out of context.

It was Hager who had spoken it, Aya finally realized. But who could blame her for having discounted the mention then, when the only useful thing the old man had said happened to sound even stranger than all the garbage that had accompanied it?

"A marvelous creature, Sitar Player," the bartender continued. "Her claiming race is today at two. You trying to make a deal with the owner?"

"If only I had a chance." Aya turned her head in anticipation.

"You must mean that little snag called financial capability." He gave a sympathetic nod. "Player will go steep, no doubt there. She will be the shining star of this track one day, mark my words. Talking about potential; I'd butcher my baby sister to have her! The guy's nuts for parting with her." He took on an impression of incredulity... "Or, on the other hand..." ...then shook it off. "Nuts!"

Another horse freak, Aya suddenly felt a prick of disappointment and closed her eyes to avoid a roll.

"Will he be taking bids in person or by proxy?" she asked, biting down on her straw in an anxious manner.

"You don't know much about how things work at the track, do you?" The bartender shook his head. "If what you're actually trying to do is get in touch with the guy, I'd check out the back lot. Tell 'em you're with Randy, they'll let you through."

"Randy? That would be you?" Aya inquired.

"Bright-eyed and bushy-tailed," the bartender bragged, declining her twenty. "Just promise to let me know how it goes." He scribbled his number on the back of a coaster.

Aya gave what she considered her toothiest smile (or was it a grimace at the appalling case of lacking self-deprecation before her). The bottom of her empty glass hit against the counter as she slid off her stool.

"Who says best thing in life aren't free?"

CHAPTER XIII

"Whatever it is you're drowning, it don't stand a chance." Someone dropped a verdict, and Wade's glazed-over pupils shifted away from the nothingness and onto the barmaid's smirk. Her round cheeks, the purple streaks in her bangs slowly drifted into focus.

"What was that?" he managed to mumble.

"It's three a.m." She smoothed out her impossibly short ponytails. "You're obviously not here to party."

Wade glanced at his half-empty glass, back at the cluster of freckles on the girl's nose, and finally around the deserted bar.

The city never sleeps, tourist slogans would have you believe. Perhaps someone should've checked out this place before stating such sweeping generalities. The damn muzak alone could put you in a coma any time of day in a matter of minutes. Thematic variety is great, no doubt, but this? An oldies retreat? Even the people on TV, acting out some dime-a-dozen tragedy, seemed to sleepwalk through their roles.

"So. What are you trying to choke?" The barmaid,

61

unmistakably top-heavy, leaned over the counter, resting her chin on her knuckles.

"Disillusionment." Wade tilted his glass to watch the light bend through the half-melted ice cubes.

"What's its name?" She was no longer trying to mask her interest by pretending to watch TV, her attention drawn exclusively to his face.

Wade paused to assess the nature of her curiosity. "No name, just a job," he replied at last.

"Oh, there's always a name." She dismissed the brush-off. "A personality conflict either starts with one or comes down to it in the end."

"A personality conflict?" Wade gave her a dirty look. "Are you trying to shrink me?"

The girl grinned as wide as she could without actually parting her lips. She must wear braces, Wade thought.

"How am I doing?"

"Lousy, lousy." With his index finger in the air, Wade drank up. "A horrendously unnatural approach."

He felt his tongue trip on double consonants.

The girl pouted. "Those were the exact words of my psych professor." Her sudden state of distress bordered on sincerity, though Wade couldn't be entirely sure which way her mood would ultimately sway.

"He said that?" Wade asked, lifting his glass as a cue for another round.

"Among other things." She fetched the bottle and gave a generous pour. "Right before he flunked me."

"I'm sorry to hear that." Basic social paradigms had to be satisfied with a word of compassion, while the barmaid nodded in a 'not your fault' sort of way. "And by the way, I didn't mean whatever I said to criticize you." The black label encouraged Wade to expand his apology. "I just wanted to be left alone."

The girl was now nodding in assent.

"Left alone, is that by any chance the reason you've been sitting here for hours, pretending to be watching Passions, knocking 'em back one after another instead of getting plastered in the solitude of your own damn room?"

"You have a point there." Wade gave it up. He would have to remember the next time around that being civil under intoxication gets you in trouble. "You really a psych student?"

"No, I'm just a bloody good bartender," she answered in a fake English accent while fixing herself a martini. "This graveyard shift is super!"

Wade gave her bow tie a lasting stare.

"I would've said drama."

"Ha-ha, very funny." She noisily sucked down every last drop of her martini and wrinkled her nose. "I'll tell you what, how about a reading?"

"A what?"

"A reading," she repeated. "Tarot. For every card of truth I turn over you owe me an answer."

Wade couldn't control a sudden burst of laughter.

"Yeah, yeah, that's what you say now." The girl didn't seem in the least bit fazed, as she produced a pack of cards, cut the deck and shuffled.

"No, no, no," Wade protested, "if you try to pass flipping cards as science, I'll have to give it to that professor of yours, he was right for failing you."

"Don't you go insulting my intelligence." The girl threw the deck down on the counter and stuck her hands on her hips. "I'm only trying to help your miserable ass. God knows why. Maybe I should just let you keep working your way toward that prospective cirrhosis, let you face your wretched fate in ignorance, huh?"

"I'm sorry, I didn't mean to…" Wade attempted to suppress his laughter. "Sorry."

"You bet your ass you are. And this, by the way," she picked the cards back up, "is an art form, and I happen to be pretty good at it."

"Okay, okay, let's do it," it was easier to comply and thus put an end to all the backtalk. "As long as you stop saying 'ass.'"

"Great. Great!" She beamed, happy as a clam. "Cut the deck for me, please. There we go."

She laid out the cards to form a cross, then picked up the one in the middle.

"This one here says you have beautiful eyes." She stretched her vowels making the word sound as 'bootiful.'

"Su-u-re," Wade mocked her technique.

"You're right, it doesn't," the girl snorted. "Though it is the truth."

"Well, thank you," Wade was too drunk and tired to address the come-on any further.

"No, it says you're troubled."

"Obviously."

"Okay." She wasn't about to give up. "Very soon, right here." She poked her finger onto a card on her left. "You'll enter a house of false heart and meet a young man you'll render service to. Hit or miss?"

House of false heart (now she sounded like a voodoo

priestess) would that be a synonym for a certain old-fashioned New York hotel? *Or am I in Louisiana instead?* Wade had to pinch himself.

"Go on." He did not give an answer.

In quick succession, the girl turned over four more cards.

"You will also meet an attractive dark-haired woman, but she's not to be trusted. Obstacles here. The Moon signifies hidden enemies, danger. There's someone else, a blonde, she's the one you seek. But the ten of wands follows, a card of false seeming. She's not what you think she is."

The barmaid paused to turn over the final card, shook it in the air.

"Your destiny." She looked at the card closely, then stuck it back into the deck without revealing its meaning.

"No, no," she muttered. "I'm not at my best today. I'd be lucky to get at least one answer out of you. One?" She pleaded.

"Alright," Wade agreed, giving in to another one of her pathetic expressions. "Just one."

It didn't take her long to come up with a question.

"Any special blondes in your life?"

"One. My partner in the Bureau," Wade replied, strangely detached, as if talking about someone on the news, someone he had never met.

"The Bureau," the girl echoed, incredulous. "As in FBI?"

"The one and only." One more trivial answer.

"What happened?" She moved up closer, overwhelmed with curiosity.

"She was discharged on the grounds of improper conduct."

"She slept with a co-worker?" the girl suggested. "You?"

Wade gave her a cold stare, trying to act offended, yet it was only an act.

"She killed someone."

"Oh," the barmaid, slightly disconcerted, backed away to fix another martini.

"A murder suspect who was sure to get away with it," Wade continued. "She went up to his house, shot him in the head and altered the scene to make it look like self-defense." Wade raised his eyebrows to emphasize the significance of the act.

"Tough mama." The girl's tone was unreadable, as she toyed with an olive. "How'd she get busted?"

"She didn't. It was her word and no evidence against it." He drew in a breath of stale air. "It's just some people thought her word wasn't good enough. Hers was a name with baggage."

"Didn't you say she practically executed a guy?"

"That guy would've walked right off the stand, screaming about police harassment, and then turned around and taken another innocent life," Wade took time to explain. "We all saw the impotence of the system; she was the only one with enough guts to do something about it."

"Were you in love with her?" The girl seemed full of tactless comments.

"Go easy on that Freudian stuff now," Wade shushed her. "We were friends. Good friends."

"And did she let her friend in on her grand plan before she went in shooting people?" Apparently shame only went so far.

"No, no she didn't. I would've tried to talk her out of it. She knew..." He swept his fingers across his field of vision, as if to put up an invisible wall. "On the other hand, I might be fooling myself entirely by thinking I could've stopped her. Maybe I'm just unable to grasp the fact that she'd never listen to anyone, her ruthless mind is too preoccupied with its own agenda, her cold heart needs no one else for sustenance."

There, he had said it, what he feared was true. But was it what he really believed? If he did, shouldn't the thought be upsetting? Wouldn't he feel angry, betrayed?

A delayed reaction taking its good old time? That was one way to look at the matter. There was also another, a more obvious explanation, and if it weren't for the present level of alcohol in his blood stream, Wade would've jumped straight to it and admitted that Aya's actions were targeted at not jeopardizing his job the way she had hers. Such a simple explanation, did he have a problem subscribing to it? Would he rather join Tieri's 'good riddance' chant than admit to gratitude? In his present state he felt hardly even fit to subscribe to Newsweek magazine.

The girl must've noticed his confusion, because her voice suddenly took on a cheerful wrap-up tone.

"Sometimes I do find hate cleansingly simple," she trilled. "Maybe it's time you introduced yourself to it."

What a strange thing to say. What a strange thing to say with a smile.

"Cheers." Wade pushed the remainder of his drink away and slid off the barstool.

"One more thing," the barmaid stopped him and reached behind the counter for the check. "Could you sign this, it's for my finals."

"Vulture." He signed without looking and threw the pen back at her.

CHAPTER XIV

First thing out of the bar Aya granted the unwanted coaster its well-deserved rest at the bottom of a trash bin and swore as her wristwatch snagged on the door.

She stepped out into the hum of the crowd outside, about to cross the stands, when a chill inexplicably ran across her back. Aya stopped dead in between two flights of stairs, suddenly aware of being watched.

She allowed her head a careful half-turn away from the sunlight to survey her surroundings.

A balding man arguing with his wife's opinion, a longhaired brunette studying the program brochure, a young businessman offering his overdressed girlfriend a drink; shrubbery, horses, jockeys. None particularly in tune with anyone else's whereabouts.

Dismissing the momentary clairvoyance, Aya resumed her journey around the stands and toward the stables.

"He's over there, prepping his horse for a warm-up." A stable boy set her on the right track and continued leaning on his shovel.

***

Out of the sun's view, the stables smelt damp and sweet. An idyllic, drowsy stillness reigned inside, only from time to time disrupted by an occasional splash of running water. An unbalanced washing machine struggled through its cycle somewhere nearby.

Aya's feet stepped on muddy straw. Her eyes filtered the shadows.

"Hey Player, ready for a stroll?" someone said, and Aya quickly hid inside the closest empty stall.

Words. Rustling noises. A discontented neigh.

Aya pulled herself up on the wooden partition of the stall and carefully peered over.

A large black horse blinking its glassy eyes, stared at a man approaching with a harness.

"Yeah, I've missed you too, girl."

The horse (was that the fabled Sitar Player?) impatiently dug its hoof into the straw dust and snorted. Its black mane scattered into the air, nostrils flared at the scent of an intruder's presence.

Not waiting to arouse the man's suspicion, Aya stepped out of the shadows.

"Ryuiji Oishi," she called out without further ado. "My name is Aya Morell. I wonder if we could have a quick word."

Oishi turned toward her. Unlike the photograph, his real face bore no sign of a smile. It seemed somewhat older for the lack of sleep, worried. His sunk-in cheeks were ever so accentuated by the idiosyncratic mop of hair. A puzzled look clouded his eyes.

Aya allowed enough time for Oishi to come to terms with her clingy corduroys and high-heel ankle boots before she spoke again. "Can we talk here or would you rather walk outside?"

"If you've come about Sitar Player, she's no longer for sale." His voice sounded somewhat uncertain as he scrutinized her face.

"So you've decided on a buyer already?" Aya asked.

"No, I've changed my mind about selling." He replaced the harness on a hook on the wall and closed the gate of his horse's stall.

"Really?" Aya made a step forward. "I guess I could say I'm sorry to hear it, but the truth is I'm not really here about the horse."

"Of course, you're not," Oishi sneered. "Anyone who knows a single thing about claiming races would ask better questions. So what is it then, Maltais considers it beneath him now to come in person?"

Aya detected a hint of an accent.

"Maybe," she said. "Or maybe I'm not here on Maltais' orders. Maybe I was just looking forward to hearing your side of the story."

"Yeah," Oishi nodded curtly, whether agreeing or as a way to express his sarcasm. "Sure. Why not. What would you like to know?" He criss-crossed his arms and leaned against the gate.

"In fear of being perceived as simple, I think I'll start with the obvious. Why did you do it?"

"Why did I do it?" Oishi scoffed, rubbing the back of his hand against his forehead. He took a deep breath as if to collect his thoughts, but instead of answering the question, he suddenly lunged at Aya, knocking her off her feet before she could get out of the way.

Not a rhetoric fan then, Aya decided as she sprung back in a practiced motion and cut Oishi's recoil short with a punch directed at his throat. The blow didn't meet its mark. Oishi backed away just in time for Aya's fist to merely slide across his jaw. He clutched at his mouth in a reflexive pain response, then let go abruptly to block Aya's next move.

Not bad for a tidy bookworm, Aya thought, reassessing Oishi's skill.

A plan of action forming as she went, Aya sunk back to the ground. She thus lured Oishi's comeback downward, and before he could realize the fatal flaw of his strategy, Aya spun around and landed a drop kick on the back of his head.

Oishi fell prone, momentarily knocked out.

Without a second's delay Aya grabbed him by the arms and dragged his body toward the stable stall. She reached under the hem of her blouse for her handcuffs and secured Oishi's wrists to the support beam. She stretched, exhaled sharply to welcome the adrenaline rush, then took out her gun and waited for Oishi to come to.

"Are we gonna behave?" Aya brought the muzzle up to his forehead.

His eyelids flew up, his arms strung taut around the beam, then went limp. He licked the blood off his lip and flashed the slightest of grins. "You have no idea what you're getting into."

"Is that so?" Aya remarked brusquely, putting the gun away. "I'll take that for a yes then."

"You're being manipulated, don't you see?" A strange emotion colored his words.

71

"Am I now?" She got up. "Is this going to be the time you tell me you're innocent, and I remind you that the window of opportunity for talking closed the moment you decided to attack me?" She walked around the beam, the heel of her boot purposely stepping on Oishi's fingers.

He grimaced in pain, yet persisted. "Why don't you call him and see for yourself? Your orders are such, aren't they? I swear, it won't be cops he'll have you deliver me to."

"He? Who's he?"

"Maltais, goddammit!" Oishi exclaimed before the nose of Aya's boot struck his ribs.

She circled another round, watching him squirm, then stopped to reach for her cell.

"Morell here. I have Oishi."

As Maltais' ready voice spoke into her ear, she was about to turn away when Oishi's legs struggled to get off the ground, his mouth opened with a shout. "No, Dannii, don't!"

CHAPTER XV

The will to breathe finally returned and Wade opened his eyes to face the world's ringing. With a grunt he turned over on his back, his hand bumping into the slumbering, (unconscious?) most definitely naked under those high thread count sheets, barmaid.

Not good. Wade couldn't even remember inviting her to his room. Or the girl's name for that matter, that is if he had actually bothered to ask for it in the first place.

He held his breath, only hoping those martinis would keep her comfortably asleep until he could sneak out to save both of them the embarrassment of dealing with his drunken amnesia.

His head leaden with a monstrous hangover, he raised his arm to check the time. Almost noon, with merciless sunlight seeping through the blinds to add aggravation to his headache. And that persistent ringing. No, not the world, only a telephone.

Wade sat up to grab the receiver.

"Mr. Wade," came a cool contralto, "you may come up now."

Unsure whether 'now' could give way to a shave and a brief

73

shower, he only took a chance on the latter to keep the nausea in check. The girl in his bed was not any less comatose than before.

"Sir," the elevator boy paid a derogatory glance to Wade's wet hair and sloppy attire.

Goddamned prim and proper piece of shit! Wade stepped inside the cage while trying the barmaid's advice on for size, considering hate for his new best friend.

"Going up," the elevator boy declared, as he pulled the metal grate door shut and cranked the gears. Upon their arrival to the penthouse, he performed the procedure in the reverse order.

"Please, come in." The unremarkable peroxide blonde inside the suite played no pretenses with politesse, her hollow apology only a soundtrack to the invitation. "I'm sorry about yesterday, but Leonard's health has been in no way suitable lately. I'm Penelope Heath, by the way, Mr. Loria's personal assistant. Is it your preference to jump into the case right away, or would you like something to drink first?"

Wade halted, searching for a place to sit. The rich palette of the interior with its honey-hued wood flooring and soaring ten-foot ceilings bespoke predictable luxury.

"A glass of water and three aspirin, if you don't mind," he said and plopped onto a leather couch.

A word was about to slip off the blonde's lips, but she turned away, taking it with her.

"Anything else?" she inquired, as he set down the empty glass, leaving a wet ring on the coffee table.

"When shall I see Mr. Loria?" Wade stretched out his legs.

"Leonard's in the bedroom getting dressed. He wished for me to break the ice." She reached for something on the desk and offered him a lacquered cherry-wood box. "Do you mind?"

Wade shook his head and received the offering.

"Inside are the notes." She preferred to remain standing, the mini-skirt of her gray suit in opposition with her conservatively pulled back hair.

Wade emptied the contents of the box into his lap and stared at the fragmented notes. Dated, accounted for, and carefully sealed in cellophane, multicolored threats, cut letter by letter out of magazine headlines. Each message began with a personal address, 'Hello Leonard,' and proceeded to a variety of comments on the theme of attention. 'Had your dose of attention today?' 'Attention-seekers will burn in hell,' 'Punishment is attention too.'

Wade ruffled through the letters. A recollection of an odd number of suspense B-movies washed over him, try as he might to resist.

"That was the first one." The blonde pointed at the note currently in Wade's hands.

"Hello Leonard. Craving some attention?" Wade read through the plastic baggie.

"We thought those might be dusted for prints." The blonde spelt out the reasoning behind the cellophane.

"Yes, of course," Wade replied numbly, apathy infiltrating his bloodstream. "Although if it's a professional we're talking about, I wouldn't get your hopes up."

He threw the notes down on the coffee table and exhaled, the atmosphere of the room suddenly oppressive. "None of these actually put forward any demands. What makes you think of blackmail?"

"The notes are but a way to break Leonard's peace of mind and make him listen." The blonde neatly folded her hands on her stomach.

"Listen to what?"

"The phone calls," she said.

"The phone calls?" Wade repeated.

"I've never actually witnessed any myself, but from what Leonard tells me, he's had at least four in the last two months. Always late at night, always the same person on the line, always the same opening statement."

"Let me guess," Wade picked the first threat note back off the coffee table.

"Hello, Leonard. Craving some attention?" The blonde read it. "Very perceptive of you, agent."

"What happens then?" Wade pressed.

"Then the person on the line says that Leonard's life will be made very uncomfortable if he doesn't cooperate. And then they hang up, without ever putting forward any demands. Until last night that is."

"What about last night?" Wade asked.

"They asked for money," the blonde said, as if the answer was too obvious to require an explanation. "One hundred thousand dollars," she added and quickly switched to lecture-like instructions. "We'd like you to fully document the drop-off. See who it is that picks up the money, follow them discretely, figure out who they work for. The drop is to take place on the corner of Carmine and Bedford."

"When?"

"An hour from now."

CHAPTER XVI

The staff nurse vacated the examining room to make way for Maltais.

"Feeling any better?" he inquired as he walked in.

His voice carried just enough consideration to stay clear of any possible accusation of criminal negligence. His eyes barely grazed over the rigid plastic cloth that covered the medical table, over Aya's limp body stretched out across it.

"As well as occipital trauma would allow." Aya cringed her headache aside and sat up, ephemeral specks flashing in her field of vision. "I seem to have been spared a concussion."

Maltais nodded impatiently to let her know he wasn't interested in further details.

"What did I miss?" Aya initiated the inevitable change of subject.

"Not anything to brag about," Maltais unbuttoned his jacket and splashed into a wood-frame chair. "Oishi has evaporated into thin air yet again, but..." He broke off, his lip bearing a smirk.

Almost undetectable, Aya thought, but certainly there. What the hell did he have to smirk about exactly? Oishi's narrow escape? The disk slipping away once more? Hardly a laughing matter.

What then? Aya's state? Aya's failure? The FBI reject falling on her ass once again; was that so amusing? Not unless Maltais had been expecting it to happen.

"That horse will be the end of him," he went on, the smirk dissipated. "It's only a matter of time. I have people now combing the surrounding area for any sightings of a horse trailer. He can't go far."

"Don't you think he'll ditch the horse?" Aya's hand involuntarily reached to check the bandage on the back of her head.

Maltais' neck turned as his eyes followed Aya's movement, but no answer ensued.

Clearly he did not find the question worthy of his valuable time and effort. Clearly, he preferred to regard Aya's opinion as irrelevant, her involvement as little more than a nuisance.

Why had he hired Aya in the first place, if her presence was so damn taxing on his composure? Some equal opportunity quota, perhaps? Some cultural competency requirement? Was that it? Was he trying to prove he was more than a simple case of closet chauvinism?

"What about Oishi's associate?" Aya asked, trying hard to suppress her agitation. "If that's what she is. Do we know anything about her identity?"

"The mysterious Dannii?" Maltais shrugged. "It would help if anybody'd actually seen her. All we have to go by is an extremely light stride and a skillful use of..." he looked bluntly amused by the idea, "…whatever she hit you with."

"They didn't take my gun," Aya noted.

"I imagine they were in a hurry," Maltais said dismissively.

"She must've searched me to get the key to the cuffs. She was bound to see the gun."

Maltais offered another shrug, his eyes increasingly vacant.

"Why hasn't Oishi left town? Or why is he back? He knows we're looking for him." Although realizing she might as well be talking to a concrete wall, Aya kept bombarding Maltais with questions.

To her surprise he answered.

"A brazen madman driven back to his kill? Dirty dealings? Perhaps, old ties. We're looking into that. Perhaps, because of this Dannii." He suddenly got up. "For now it would be wise to keep every possibility open."

Before walking out Maltais halted, his eyes stopped on Aya's face as if in a flash of some unforeseen realization.

"The nurse informed me you'd require some rest." He wrinkled his nose. "Stitches and all. Take as long as you need to recover, I'll give you a call as soon as anything comes to surface."

CHAPTER XVII

Biding his time with a cup of chicory coffee Wade watched Loria's 528i pull out of the taxicab stampede and into the bus lane.

Loria himself, wearing black from head to toe, emerged out of the driver's seat. His hand, unsteady yet determined, lowered a crumpled brown bag inside a municipal trash bin.

Wade recognized that slouched anorexic figure, though thus far he only knew it from the front cover of Fortune magazine, so graciously showcased by Ms. Heath.

"Leonard is under too much pressure right now to manage a formal introduction. The new real estate project, the media, all too much in his current state," she explained, as she ushered Wade out of the penthouse, down to the lobby and into a taxi waiting out by the curb.

"You have your instructions," she addressed the cabby and slammed the car door shut.

The world fell away. The noise, the streets had disappeared into a moment of confusion. Wade found himself unable to connect with what was real.

Whoever Fights Monsters

What was he supposed to be doing exactly? What miracle of investigative trade was he expected to perform? Just like that, straight out of bed, unprepared. Thrown naked into the icy water.

"We'd like you to fully document the drop." No camera? No vehicle? No sunglasses. Even Wade's cell phone had been left behind on the charger in his hotel room.

Or was it the whole point, that carelessness, and Miss Overprotective Assistant knew there would be absolutely nothing to document?

Was it Loria himself who had written those letters and hired someone to make the phone calls? If there even were any phone calls. Or was it all a mere cry for attention, just like the letters said?

But if Heath knew all that already, why the charade? Why not say it up front? Was she being monitored in some way? By Loria? To make sure she didn't misbehave? After all, Tieri did mention Loria's growing distrust toward her.

She knew her own word wouldn't weigh much, certainly not enough to discourage Loria's schizophrenic tendencies, so she decided to play along. To acquire an expert opinion from a neutral party.

Tieri had hit the bull's eye. All Wade had to do was get those paranoias cleared. Was that all there was to it? Oh yes, not missing any fun in the meantime, of course. He seemed to be moving along nicely in the fun department. Fun. Right.

Wade bit down on an ice cube and followed Loria's 528 off with his unenthusiastic eyes. No tinted glass, he noticed. Surely one of the blackmailer's so-called demands. The victim must act alone.

Wade picked out the next ice cube to chew on (keeps a man awake). The sidewalk in front of the café now swarmed with the late lunch crowd. Streaming by. Surging by like disjointed moments in life. Someone else's life.

And as the waiting game commenced, among that sea of commotion Wade suddenly spotted an embodiment of calm.

Knotted black hair, blood-red tight-fitting tank top, bare midriff, narrow leather-clad hips. She stood, statuesque, against the granite wall across the road, a cigarette dying away in her long manicured fingers. A vision? A demon? In tune with the crowd, yet screaming of an out of beat plea to differ.

Careless, she flickered away the cigarette and dove into the human sea to pay her dues to the three-eyed traffic beast. Her feet connected confidently with the two-tone crosswalk.

Wade saw her reach inside the trash bin to retrieve her prize, but instead of walking away afterwards, the girl suddenly halted.

A moment of unmistakable astonishment raced through her dark eyes before Wade even had a chance to fully exit the cafe. She turned around, as if expecting to see him there. Before Wade knew what was happening, she stuck the bag behind her belt and, with a gazelle-like jolt, took off.

Avoiding the moving obstacles in her way, the girl ran hard down the racetrack of the city streets toward Downing. Nearly colliding with a career party exiting Phil's Pizza, she jumped over the side of the subway entrance and slid down the polished handrail.

Wade kept up, ready to close in as he rushed down the stairs. He saw the girl look back briefly just before, without a sign of hesitation, she hopped the turnstiles. Just before Wade was sideswiped by the violently perturbed security guard.

And that was it. The vision evaporated. The demon got away unscathed.

Wade flashed his badge.

"Out of the way!"

But his 'Hold the doors' arrived too late to keep the train from slithering off into the pitch-black tunnel.

CHAPTER XVIII

Aya slipped her hands between the sliding doors before they had a chance to converge. The gear assembly made a sharp grinding sound and forced the doors back into the jamb.

"Neuetech couldn't splurge on some grease?" Aya stepped inside the elevator cab in time to catch the look of excruciating boredom slip off Ronnie Halprin's face.

"Officer," he swallowed hard, as if about to choke.

"Ronnie," Aya acknowledged his presence with a nod and verified his floor selection as matching her own.

"Working Sundays also?" she asked, thus adding another link to the chain of seeming coincidences.

"Chasing the mighty nickel." Ronnie gave a strained chuckle. "Unknown domain on terminal 141 today, universe to be saved tomorrow. Doing all right yourself?"

Despite the attempted exercise in wit, Ronnie looked somewhat self-conscious. He fidgeted, his smile turning inept, as he gave a cautious glance to the dry mud on Aya's pants. "Managing?"

"Doing great, Ronnie, great." Aya kept herself braced for one of Ronnie's loquacious streaks to kick in. "Reaping those comforting effects of Demerol."

But his aloofness remained in place even after she awarded herself with a slap on the backside. *What gives?*

"They say it can impede one's judgment, Demerol," she went on, puzzled over the nature of Ronnie's inexplicably altered demeanor. "What d'you think? Am I okay to drive?"

Ronnie looked up from Aya's mud-stained attire with a dazed expression.

Was there something Aya had failed to detect before? Some dark demons she was setting off? What was it now? Claustrophobia, mysophobia, incorrectly administered meds? Fear of god's punishment for working on a day of worship? A dead grandma in the mix? Aya started to inquire, but before her words of concern had time to form, the elevator arrived at its ground floor destination, jerking Ronnie out of his apparently pained state.

"I'd be more than glad to offer you a ride," he stuttered through a belated reply.

"Really?" Aya stepped out into the lobby, Ronnie sheepishly following her lead. "I'm not one to interfere with people's plans."

"No, no plans," he assured. "I was only going home to have dinner, feed my cat."

"Well then, perhaps we could do better," she suggested. "How would a couple of tequila shots sound to you?"

"Great," Ronnie abandoned his tailgating position and hurried past Aya to hold the front door open.

"Great!" he said again with a slightly higher dose of confidence.

CHAPTER XIX

Aya changed into a pair of cropped jeans and a fresh T, and peeled the bandage off her head to seek the miracles of comb-over, armed with a tube of styling gel and a diffuser.

What was up with Ronnie anyway, her mind kept wondering as she worked her fingers through her hair. He certainly was acting odd.

Was he on something? Psychotropics? Perhaps the man was bipolar.

If Ronnie's character was truly unstable, then getting him involved might be a mistake.

Was it too late to back out, the conservative in Aya asked. Of course not, the bold innovator came back to answer without a second's delay. No such thing as too late. So why play it safe? Ronnie was perfect after all, in so many ways. He was there, already waiting in the bar.

Aya put away the diffuser and slipped her feet into satin high-heel slides, the only touch of extravagance to counterweigh her otherwise casual attire.

Whoever Fights Monsters

When had she ever been one to dwell on hesitation?

***

"Doing okay?" Aya landed on a stool next to Ronnie's, the final drops of her recent indecision having evaporated on her way down from her hotel room.

Besides, Ronnie's attitude seemed to have swung back to its extravert side as he beamed, "Terrific!" and pointed at the extra glass on the bar counter. "Your drink."

Aya downed the alcohol in one gulp, almost convinced Ronnie's metamorphoses were just a figment of her drugged imagination.

"Only on a day like this," she exhaled. "Medicinal purposes."

"Medicinal?" Ronnie asked, skeptically. "Is that *with* Demerol or without?"

"You tell *me* the next time you get hit on the head."

"Is that what happened to you?"

"More or less," Aya sank her teeth into a slice of lime and puckered up. "Maltais would probably call it a cat fight. Without so much of a fight that is."

Ronnie regarded her, somewhat perplexed.

"The bitch snuck up from behind," Aya provided the explanation he needed.

"I'm sorry."

"Just a professional hazard, I'm afraid," Aya signaled for another round. "But hell, I can order anything off the menu free of charge. Well worth the risk, I was led to believe. Bottoms up?" She raised her shot glass and watched Ronnie fumble with his.

"So what about you?" Aya went on. "Let's talk about you.

You enjoy your job. You're good at your job."

"Enough education and dedication," Ronnie's tongue was coming unwound in direct co-relation with the number of tequila shots consumed.

"Another," Aya waved to the bartender, while Ronnie bragged.

"Once in a while there's a call for a certain level of creativity, but mostly routine stuff. Nothing a trained monkey couldn't manage."

"By creativity you mean being resourceful and clever." A man's ego, unlike his focus, had never been known to suffer from a pinch of flattery.

"Those exact qualities that separate men from monkeys." Ronnie eagerly accepted her praise, ready to admit his own brilliance at any given time.

"Right," Aya nodded, moving on. "Would you say then that Oishi's case required creativity?"

"The technological part of it, I'll say. But what do I know about the workings of criminal mentality." He made a helpless gesture and finished off his drink.

Aya's unseeing eyes mechanically scanned the bar, her mind craving to make a discovery.

Was there a sense to that symbiosis of lacquer and oak around her? The symmetrical outlines of objects and people basking in penumbra? The incoherent tune of human voices? Ronnie's wide-eyed gaze resting upon her face?

And that's when it hit her, could it not? Could it be any more obvious? It all suddenly made perfect sense. Ronnie's behavior, the cause of his mood swings. How could she have not recognized the telltale signs before?

"What if I say there's something I'd like you to take a look at." A plan of action was shaping up in Aya's head as she spoke. "A video recording."

Ronnie's reaction was quick. "So it exists," he gasped.

"Beg your pardon?" Aya downplayed her level of intelligence.

"The fabled surveillance footage, it exists after all. I have to admit I've been guilty of entertaining some doubts," he sniffed. "The Security Department does not exactly offer the rest of us an open channel of communication. I don't mean you, of course. I mean Maltais and his guard dogs. I could never imagine having a drink with Maltais or..." His curiosity peaked mid-sentence. "You do have it? The tape?"

Aya reached into her back pocket and produced the video surveillance disk from Oishi's case file. "What do you say?" She gave it a shake.

Ronnie's hand started toward the disk, then froze half way. "By saying you want me to look at it, you don't actually mean just looking, do you?" he said, as the reality of the matter dawned upon him. "You want my professional opinion. You want me to use Neuetech's computer lab and analyze the data, don't you?"

Aya neither denied nor confirmed his supposition.

"I don't think I'm really the right person to ask," Ronnie said after a long pause. "I replace power cords and printer cartridges. I'm not exactly an expert on video imaging."

What had just happened to being creative, resourceful and clever, Aya wondered, confused by Ronnie's sudden reluctance.

"There's no need for false modesty," she reassured him.

"No, it's not that." He shook his head. "It's just I would rather not get involved with security issues. It's not really my place. Or my job. Please, don't misunderstand; I'd love to help. But I don't want any trouble. Just have Maltais call me, I'll explain."

Ronnie looked so incredibly uncomfortable, Aya thought he was about to slip into squirming. That little coward, she finally recognized his reluctance for what it really was and interrupted his ramblings.

"Ronnie, Ronnie," she chanted, not about to be dismissed so easily. If Ronnie wasn't going to help her willingly, then she would just have to make him. Of course, she could forget all about him and take the disk to a professional, but that would mean having to wait till tomorrow, and Aya was not in the habit of wasting time.

"I told Maltais you were okay." She decided to skip the niceties and proceeded with the final measure.

"What do you mean?" Ronnie's pupils were still clouded from evasion when he looked up.

"He had doubts about your level of competency, so he asked me to look into it."

Ronnie's expression was still as blank as the color of his T-shirt, while he waited for Aya to spell it out.

"He thought you were drinking on the job." Aya paused to let her words sink in. "I told him he was wrong. He is wrong, isn't he?"

Aya knew all too well Maltais wouldn't give a dead horse's testicles about some nerdy employee with a drinking problem. Petty staffing issues were none of his concern. He wouldn't dream to stoop that low, and Aya felt almost guilty for telling Ronnie otherwise. Almost. But not enough to lose sight of her objective. The end result justified the means.

Ronnie looked at his empty glass, back at Aya's face.

"Of course." His chin slightly trembled. "Of course he's wrong."

"So why don't you work with me, and we can get him off your back once and forever? What do you say?" She held out the disk once again.

CHAPTER XX

Ronnie popped the surveillance disk into the ROM drive and waited for the data to load.

"Play," he announced, hitting a key, and a sequence of black and white images filled the screen.

They were the same images Aya had seen a number of times before. A man in a white coat, swiftly crossing the familiar ChD lab floor; leaning over a terminal to perform a series of rushed manipulations, alternated by long periods of waiting; exiting the scene with the same haste that marked his arrival. Aya didn't know what it was, but she sensed that something was amiss.

Perhaps, if she could see it with fresh eyes. If the entire order of events weren't etched into her memory. Maybe then she could put her finger on what it was that bothered her. Perhaps, it was something too minute for her conscious mind to register, something that her laptop with its limited capabilities couldn't bring up.

Aya looked at Ronnie, as he fidgeted at his desk, inside the tech support home base. His computer made a whirring sound before starting the recording over, with playback switched into frame-by-frame function.

"Well, that's Oishi all right," Ronnie declared halfway through the second run.

"Can you tell what he's doing right here?" Aya pointed to the shadow of Oishi's lab coat.

Ronnie backtracked, waiting for Aya's signal.

"Right here," she gestured. "He's gonna turn his head. Freeze that."

Ronnie complied with a click of the mouse.

"He's downloading something, no doubt about it." He upped the level of magnification. "Looks like gibberish, doesn't it?" After a slight pause, Ronnie nodded, as if answering his own question. "It's encrypted. A list of file names in all likelihood. And this bar in the middle, barely beginning to fill in..."

"Maltais did say a truckload," Aya noted.

"You bet." Ronnie resumed normal playback. "Can't see much like this, can you? The whole thing is sort of fuzzy."

"One would expect better quality lenses from an industrial giant."

"Well, there're all sorts of explanations for this kind of distortion," Ronnie suggested.

"Such as?" Aya urged him to go on.

"Anything as bizarre as solar activity or as simple as sloppy duplication."

"Duplication. Meaning this recording is a copy?"

"Oh, it most certainly is, but that's..." Ronnie started, but Aya interrupted him.

"Has it been tampered with?"

"I'm not saying no." Ronnie shook his head pensively. "I'm

not saying yes either. I honestly don't know how one would tell. Besides, what would be the point of doing something like that?"

Ronnie waited for a possible hypothesis to come, but Aya never supplied one. She only kept staring, expressionless, at the screen, until Ronnie followed her example.

"Do this part frame by frame again," she finally said. "No, no, go back a little first. Here."

It was a while before an indefinable sound escaped Ronnie's throat.

"You see that?" He hit pause, then selected a field for magnification. "The reflection in the adjacent monitor."

"What is that?" Though close proximity made the image even hazier, Aya involuntarily drew closer.

"Looks like a wall plate," Ronnie adjusted the contrast and gave a clap of satisfaction. "Thank god for plain black screen savers."

"L-2," Aya read. "What does that mean?"

"It means," Ronnie's face turned grave from the monumental realization. "The room we're looking at is not, in fact, the room that houses Oishi's lab. An honest mistake to make, all the rooms here look like clones. That's how Neuetech likes them, all neat and standardized."

"So you've seen that plate before?"

"Oh no, you misunderstand. There's not a plate like that here. Not in this building," Ronnie said with certainty. "And my humble duties have taken me anywhere there is a hard drive."

"L-2?" Aya tested all variations for plausibility. "Lab 2? Level 2?"

Ronnie shook his head. "Not here."

For a minute Aya felt stumped, her mind racing in circles.

Yet she managed to bring forth a change of subject. "Get me wiring schematics for this building," she prompted.

Ronnie stared, hesitant. "I'm not sure that's a good... I don't think I'm really allowed..." Ronnie's cautious consideration didn't take long to buckle under Aya's silent scrutiny.

With a groan, he double-clicked the service folder. "I can only guess at what it is you're looking for, but trust me, you won't find it here."

Aya took the mouse out of Ronnie's deliberately faltering hand and scrolled down to the basement plans.

"The only villains one might run into there are sour mop heads and rat poison."

Ronnie's skepticism was becoming increasingly distracting, as Aya tried to shuffle her deck of working theories. "Show me Neuetech's standing orders," she demanded.

Ronnie ran a quick search, all his declarations of futility stifled. "No, no mention of any L-2s."

"Can I see the whole list?" Aya asked taking over the mouse once again. "These are on a monthly basis?"

"Bi-weekly," Ronnie corrected. "Why?"

"C_8H_{18}," Aya read incredulously. "They order 2,500 gallons of gasoline bi-weekly? You'd figure that's a little excessive."

"Refined?" Ronnie took the lack of an answer as a yes and rubbed the back of his neck, puzzled. "Not anything they'd use in plastics then. Not in those quantities anyway. We do have some company cars, but they don't fuel them on site."

"In that case, I'm afraid, there's no other way to find out," Aya exhaled and pulled away from Ronnie's chair.

"What are you doing?" Ronnie's pupils widened, as she reached for the phone.

"Making a call to the vendor," Aya said. "Hopefully they keep a temp or two to answer their phones on week-ends."

"Wait, wait!" Ronnie's voice pained to differ. "Do we absolutely have to use this phone? If anyone finds out... We should try a payphone."

"I fear this wouldn't be nearly as effective without the company caller signature." Aya began punching in the numbers from the bottom of the supply list. "And if we get busted, you know you'd lay all the blame on me anyway, right?" She slipped in a playful wink. "Tell them I threatened you with your life, they'll shade in the grays."

"I wouldn't..." Ronnie began, just as the call had gone through.

Aya pressed her finger to her lips, a sign for the positively traumatized Ronnie to shut up.

"Yes, hi," she spoke into the receiver. "My name is Kimberly Wells, I'm a junior accountant with the Southwest office of Neuetech Industries. Yes, working overtime. I'm afraid we've come across a discrepancy in our monthly report." Aya sat down on Ronnie's desk and played with the phone cord while the operator pulled up the accounts. "I need to verify the latest delivery... Yes." Aya snapped her fingers at Ronnie's pen and used the back of her hand as a note-pad. "Thank you. We're getting it all cleared up." Aya hung up enjoying the look of anticipation of doom on Ronnie's face.

"Thank god for temporary office workers." She finally broke the suspense. "A very nice lady has just informed me that the delivery in question had been made to a location at North I-17 and New River Road."

"Well done," Ronnie coughed out with clear relief.

"Does Neuetech have an affiliate north of Phoenix?" Aya wouldn't let him bask in his newly acquired tranquility for long.

Ronnie frowned at what he saw was unavoidably coming, then embraced the inevitable by repeating Aya's earlier words.

"There's no other way to find out, is there?"

CHAPTER XXI

"Behold the bearer of good news!" The receiver crackled, a voice on the other side fading in and out.

"All ears." Wade tried for the short and sweet to avoid a sermon on employee under-appreciation and ways to bury one's brilliance in a bacteria-infested basement in Quantico, where poor cell-phone reception comes with the paycheck. All the above otherwise known as conversation starters if you happened to know Lloyd.

Everybody in DC knew Lloyd. And his Welsh ancestry. And his poodle Mickey. And his wife Jennifer who couldn't cook to save her life. And his obnoxious stepbrother Joe who was constantly in debt.

Yes, that Lloyd, the evidence room clerk. The king of 'I'll wash your back just to hear the latest developments in your life story.' The lord of 'secrets can't be kept forever, might as well be the one to put those puppies out there.' The czar of 'my wife starves me so, I'll do anything for free take-out.' That Lloyd who was now rephrasing the suspect's description that Wade had given him.

"Female. Mixed ethnicity. Early to mid twenties. Five foot seven. A hundred and twenty pounds, thereabouts. Black hair. Dark eyes. Attractive.

Wade was quite sure he heard sniggering.

"Distinguishing features..."

"A tattoo in the shape of a line of black cats, stretching from the back of her right ear to her seventh vertebra," Wade finished the sentence, impatient. "Name!"

"My friend, you don't love me. You only use me for my connections upstairs," Lloyd whined off-topic. "And what happened to that postcard I've been promised?"

"Name," Wade repeated sternly.

"Jessica Ann Katz. Happy now?" There was a definite chuckle this time.

"Absolutely. You're a fucking magician. Buying you lunch is the first thing on my to-do list."

"Schlotzky's the word, buddy. Now here comes the bio." Crackling increased, as Lloyd hammered at the scroll key. "Born 1979, parents not known. Brought up in foster homes. A high-school dropout. One and only arrest and conviction in 1996. Grand theft auto. Out on parole in six months. No illegal activity on record since. Or activity of any sort for that matter. Big sorry there. But I do have a lovely mug shot here, got a fax number?"

Lloyd waited for the answer, then cleared his throat and drawled, "So-o-o, enjoying the nightlife, Wade?"

"Doing my best, Lloyd."

Wade felt a surge of belated relief. He slouched down on a bar stool, switched hands holding the receiver and looked around. Just some coffee shop, the city seemed full of them. Just a nameless place he stumbled upon as he walked destination-free away from the subway station. A place to get lunch, make some calls, reassess his view of the matters at hand.

"Say hi to Jessica for me, would you?" Lloyd said hopefully.

"I'm afraid we're not exactly on speaking terms," Wade was eager to disappoint.

"Listen buddy." Lloyd picked up his pace. "After the grand total of three years of you bringing me loose body parts and occasional deli products, I have found out from sources most secure that the only female whose company you've shared outside of work lately is a dyke. A most hot one, I'll give you that, but nevertheless, dangerously psycho. Oh yes, you're right, I'm walking on the eggshells of the loving memory of Aya Morell here."

Lloyd inhaled laboriously. "There's plenty others out there, you know. A good-looking guy like you? They'd hurl themselves at you if you let 'em. As clear in my mind as this damn leaking freezer. As a friend, don't throw it away on something never to be had." Lloyd paused, then added almost desperately, "And for Pete's sake, send me that postcard!"

CHAPTER XXII

Wade reviewed the facts.

Fact number one – whether staged or real, the blackmail money drop had taken place.

Number two – Jessica Ann Katz *was* a convicted felon.

Three – Penelope Heath's behavior seemed most odd.

Then came the questions.

One – Was that money drop all it had seemed to be?

Two – Did Loria know Jessica? Did he hire her to assist with his delusional scheme? If so, to what purpose? Was there a purpose?

Three – Did Ms. Heath know the truth about what was going on? Was she somehow involved in the blackmail? Or was she simply too familiar with Loria's eccentricities to buy into the existence of any real malice against him? Was there something else to her relationship with Loria Wade didn't know?

Four – Why couldn't Wade stop being a perfectionist and get on with his life?

Before leaving the bar Wade glanced around one last time,

his attention drawn by an after work party of nine-to-fivers. Office assistants, no doubt, all female. Cosmetics and trendy clothes, making up for what wasn't there in beauty. Whispers of a conversation. Stifled laughs around a bowl of punch. The redhead in a striped jacket, was she looking at him? Or past him? Was she waving to him? Was she getting up to approach him? Wade wasn't about to stay and find out. He threw a twenty on the counter and hastily walked out.

CHAPTER XXIII

"Shit, that's a gas station." Aya brought Ronnie's fully loaded Accord to a sudden stop, a dust cloud rising from the back tires.

Ronnie exhaled (relieved again?) and pulled the seatbelt away from his neck. "The mystery of excessive orders solved."

Abandoning her customary reserve, Aya let a short stream of resentment escape her lips and hit the steering wheel with both hands.

Ronnie jumped in his seat.

"Why would a company like Neuetech own a gas station?" Aya demanded.

"Hell, why not!" Ronnie's gaze was still on the steering wheel, perhaps to make sure the part sustained no damage. "I thought about going into that business myself once. Profit margins not spectacular, but income is steady."

Ronnie's mouth was already open to bring forth another pearl of traditional wisdom, when he finally caught Aya's reproving look and turned sulky.

"But, of course, that's not what you are driving at."

Aya leaned over the car's central console and pulled her binoculars out of the glove box.

"Middle of nowhere." She brought the binoculars up to her eyes. "Hot as blazes. Nothing but Joshua trees. And, if you haven't noticed, not an electric pole in sight."

"Laying cable's expensive," Ronnie threw out an estimate. "Remote places like that use a generator."

Aya released the clutch to let the car creep up closer toward a shallow drainage ditch, until the front wheels halted at the edge of a low bridge. They were now less than thirty yards away from the structure. Aya hoped the concrete enclosure of the bridge would keep them concealed.

She killed the engine, rolled down the windows and stuck her head outside. "One hell of a quiet generator."

The building seemed deserted. Aya looked at its bleached walls, its dark, still windows, almost expecting to spot a ghostly apparition.

"Well, they'd keep the thing buried to muffle the sound," came another moment-breaking supposition from Ronnie.

"We'll see about that." Aya removed the binoculars from her lap, set them on the dash and leaned back against the headrest.

From above the rims of her sunglasses she saw Ronnie's expression, uneasy with expectation.

Most men find themselves challenged by the passive act of waiting, Aya remembered. That insuppressible urge to go out there, kick ass, or whatever they imagined real life should require. The urge, deeply lodged in every part of their being, was now eating away at Ronnie.

Aya realized she should pick a topic for a conversation before Ronnie had a chance to. She shuddered to think of what he might come up with. His favorite brand of underwear, if he could get away with it. More excitement from the memoirs of a techie.

"So Ronnie, how do you normally spend your Sunday nights? No wife? Girlfriend?"

"Divorced," he answered concisely.

"Hmm." Aya faked a grunt of concern.

"Being married to your job means coming home to find your wife's suitcases packed and your less diligent colleague loading them into his SUV," Ronnie's voice degraded into genuine torment, as he spoke.

The human ability to feel, such a strange contraption, Aya thought. The depth of sentiment, nothing but a time bomb lying in wait until someone, something trips the trigger. Embrace that inner self, and you'll find yourself standing amid a minefield with no direction safe enough to take. No direction but the structured void of immediate tasks and goals that render the triggering mechanism dormant, as basic reactions of fear, joy and sorrow are being suppressed without consideration, for the sole sake of the clarity of mind.

Aya had no time to waste on failure or self-loathing. No room for torment and regret.

"Tough break," she whispered and in that single second felt almost envious of Ronnie's neuroses and sensitivities and Gavin's broken heart. Their surrender to imperfections, their weaknesses. That human desire for a kindred spirit, was she in search of one herself?

Her thoughts wandered, but only for a moment. "No kids?" she asked.

"Only Pinky, the cat, over whom I got full custody, it seems.

Laurel and I had only been married four months," Ronnie's hand made a chopping motion. "What about you?"

Aya looked up to realize that Ronnie had picked up on her reluctance to talk of her personal life, and she hated him for making the fact obvious.

"It's getting windy," she said, as if Ronnie's question never existed. "Must be the sunset."

She pushed her glasses back up to her eyes and pointed to a distant speck on the horizon.

"First one on the road ever since we've been here. Care for a bet? Ten bucks says he's pulling off."

The silver contour of a semi finally separated from the sunset and, its speed decreasing, signaled a turn. As it jumped the curb, a soft drink logo flickered across its side.

"A refrigeration car," Aya commented, while Ronnie fished out a stick of gum from his pocket.

"Delivering soda on a Sunday night," Ronnie chewed, concluding the sentence.

"Probably so, but what if..." Aya didn't finish. She took the key out of the ignition and swung the car door open.

After taking a few steps along the cracked asphalt, she turned around. "If I'm not back in a couple of hours, leave. Call the police. Tell them everything you know."

She dropped the key in the empty driver's seat.

Anxious, Ronnie licked his dry lips and gave a quick nod.

CHAPTER XXIV

Aya made an earnest effort to take a roundabout route to remain undetected as she jumped into the dry ditch that cut through the open desert beside the gas station.

The semi driver was now getting out of the truck, unlocking the back hatch and extending the ramp.

Hunched over, Aya walked along the rocky bottom of the ditch until she could no longer see the storefront. Before crossing the distance toward the sidewall of the building she looked back at Ronnie's Honda, now almost completely hidden in the shadows of the bridge.

And then she darted.

Visits to the gym always pay off in the end. Aya didn't even need to catch her breath when she reached the building. Only then did she notice a dusty Chevy parked in the narrow back lot under the 'staff only' sign on the wall. So there was an employee inside after all.

She heard the front door of the store chime and peeked cautiously around the corner of the building. The driver was now joined by the store clerk, both hardly seeing beyond the small task of prepping the loading dock.

Aya saw her chance as both men disappeared behind the truck's body.

"I've got a little something for you personally," the driver shouted to the clerk.

A split moment was enough for Aya to slip past them and onto the loading platform.

***

The cramped storage area would not get on the good side of the housekeeper of the month committee. Aya shrugged the soiled rubber flaps of the curtains out of the way and gave the out-of-order sign on the padlocked restroom door a hurried glance.

With no time to spare, she moved behind the crates full of potato chips and toilet tissue and crouched down, her back to the dust bunnies of the concrete wall.

She did not have to wait long. The sound of nonchalant voices, the smell of weed and a whiny tune of a two-wheeled dolly cut through the heavy air.

Aya held her breath, her hands slippery around the Kimber, and watched the driver's fatigued performance, his pudgy face breaking a sweat as he leaned the dolly against the wall and ran a hand through his matted hair.

Instead of unloading the dolly, the driver approached the restroom door. He undid the padlock and pushed his burden through, down a dimly lit hallway beyond.

Aya seized her opportunity before the door could slam shut

and followed him.

As the locking mechanism clicked behind her, there came a quick succession of electronic beeps and the low hum of automated lights picture-framed the short stretch of the corridor ahead, a freight elevator at its end.

"No need to turn around." Aya's voice rang hollow, the weight of the Kimber's barrel now resting against the driver's ear. "Now, what do we say you put your loyalties aside and continue as you would on your merry way."

The driver stood speechless; his hand twitched, then hesitantly reached toward a metal box mounted on the wall beside the elevator. He flipped the cover to reveal a key code lock within.

Aya watched him punch in a string of digits, then place his thumb on the return pad to make the elevator doors slide open.

"Fingerprint scan," she noted. "Fancy. Now let's pick up those boxes, we don't want them to look out of place, do we?"

The driver clutched at the dolly and pulled it into the cab.

A matching lock was mounted inside as well, and Aya waved the gun, inviting the driver to engage the scan. The door slid back into the closed position and the elevator began its downward progression.

"Shouldn't we talk about what's down below?" Aya prompted the driver, who stood with his jaws soldered shut with terror, the smell of sweat evident in such close quarters.

"What's the matter? Cat got your tongue? You were conversing beautifully to your friend there just minutes ago. Or are you shy with the ladies?"

The elevator's journey came to its end, and the doors opened into a fairly large chamber, empty, but for a number of rectangular support columns.

No surveillance cameras that she could see. Aya pushed her captive out onto the gray concrete slab floor, cool air tingling at her bare ankles. She looked around, puzzled by the absence of additional entryways.

"What the hell is this?" she addressed the driver, only to have him back away toward the tile wall and slide down to the floor, his face drained of all color.

Aya spun around, frustrated. "What's in the boxes?" she demanded.

She took out a knife from under her belt with the intention of cutting open the boxes, when the driver emitted a wail of panic.

"I'm not gonna cut you, you silly bastard," she said with a note of irritation in her voice. "Not right this moment at least." Aya put away the knife and approached the driver gently. "What's your name, pal?"

"Phillip." He swallowed with apparent difficulty, his pupils dilated. "I have a wife and two children."

"Sure you do," Aya dismissed the plea. "But if you don't start working on your communication, Phillip, I'll be forced to slit your throat, chop off your thumbs and do some experimenting on my own."

She gave a short pause to let the picture sink in. "Or I could start on your thumbs first, whichever you prefer. Do you think anyone would hear you scream?"

"The elevator goes farther down, but I don't have the pass code," the driver spat out laboriously.

"You're not helping," Aya reintroduced the knife into the conversation and gave it a flip. "What's in the boxes?"

"Nothing. Supplies," he choked.

"So which one is it? Nothing? Or supplies?"

"Supplies."

"What kind of supplies?"

"Food, stationery, cleaning provisions." He wiped the sweat off his eyelids.

"Who picks them up?"

"I don't know, they come up after I leave," he faltered.

"What's down there?" Aya squatted in front of him.

"I don't know; I've never been further than this room."

"Did it never strike you that it was suspicious to have a high security cell underneath a gas station?"

"It's none of my business. For all I know it's some rich psycho with extended family. For all I know it's the government."

"Who hired you?"

"I'm subcontracting for a transport company." The driver swallowed again, then added fervently. "What do you want?"

Aya ignored his question. "How often do you make drop-offs here?"

"Twice a week." The sprint of emotion made the driver's voice hoarse.

"Always at this hour?"

The driver nodded.

The knife still in her hand, Aya sat down on the floor beside him. "Then we'll just have to sit here and wait for them to come up and introduce themselves, won't we?"

CHAPTER XXV

"What the hell were you thinking?! You were clearly told not to interfere!" Fury distorted the blonde's nondescript features, as she shielded the doorway with her outstretched arm. "Which means the blackmailer was not to be confronted. And now we've had another call...."

"How about Mr. Loria and I talk?" Wade pushed Heath's arm down and walked past her inside the penthouse and toward the bedroom.

The door was ajar.

An emaciated man in silk pajamas was resting against the headboard of a four-poster bed, his body propped by a number of oddly shaped pillows, his hair dark, wiry and hardly an object of a barber's care of late. But perhaps, that was mode du jour in his circles. Whatever circles those might have been, they at least seemed to encourage clean-shaven faces.

A series of TV screens, built into the wall in front of the bed, relayed partial images from the living room. The man put aside his copy of Wolfram's Philosophical Logic and gave a weak imitation of a smile, his colorless eyes measuring Wade up and down.

"An impressive gadget, isn't it?" Loria pointed at the flickering monitors. "Its sole purpose being to capture the life I could never have. Just look at them all." He switched the feed into the camera in the lobby. "Aren't they precious?"

The screen filled with images of dinnertime bustle. "Their little problems, their little thrills."

Loria switched the feed again, this time into the Old Days bar. He must've detected Wade's unease at the sight, for he rushed to explain. "Don't worry, Agent. No privacy invasion here. No secrets learned. At least not the kind that slip off someone's lips. Just a study in facial expressions, gestures. Body language, a tongue in its own right."

Loria zoomed in on the sugary grin of a hostess, then on the unequivocally positioned middle finger, she tried to hide behind her clipboard.

"What are words but impediments?"

"Tieri sends his regards." Wade was not a particular fan of head games.

"Nice to meet you as well, Agent." Loria hit the screen saver, his failed attempt to impress giving way to sarcasm. "I do remember him mentioning your exceptional competence."

"What does she have on you?" Cutting to the chase never felt better.

"Pardon me? She?" Loria raised his almost hairless brow.

"Jessica Ann Katz." Wade produced a blurry fax mug shot and held it out for Loria to see.

"Never met her in my entire life."

The answer came a little too quickly.

"A trash can. Quite a tired idea, don't you find?" Wade

commented. "One of your own?"

Loria went for a defensive gesture, but Wade never gave him a chance to speak.

"One hundred thousand dollars, I'd put on some extortionist theatrics for that myself. That's assuming she's keeping the whole amount. A few letters, phone calls, a nice display out there in the street. Easy as pie. I say the girl is overpaid."

"If you're implying..." Anxious, Loria rose off the pillows, but again Wade cut him short.

"Who would blackmail a notoriously wealthy man such as yourself for a grand sum of one hundred thousand dollars, an amount hardly exceeding your annual underwear bill? What kind of an extortionist in their right mind would put on a red outfit and loud make-up to pick up the drop instead of trying to blend in? What is it you were seeking? Attention? Compassion? Ms. Heath knows the whole story surely."

"Dear Penelope." Loria suddenly regained his calm. "That's been her view all along, you know." He chuckled. "I see she wasn't too shy to share it with you. Dear Penelope."

He slapped his hands against the bed throw.

"We shared a… what you'd call a fling some time ago, she and I. She's a nice enough girl, but a bit too obsessive for my taste. I had to break it off. I see she's still under a delusion that my well-being relies solely upon her. I should've let her go, I suppose. But she knows her job well, she's dedicated, and I don't have to get used to someone new all over again.

"Penelope seems to be, though she won't say it to my face, under a wrongful impression that I, for whatever reason, have hired someone to stage an act of blackmail. Can you believe it?!" Loria scoffed. "Oh yes, of course, you already do. But what you should also believe is there are things Penelope does not and should never know."

"So what you're saying is the extortion case is real."

"You got it, cowboy." Unlike his choice of words, Loria's voice was flat.

"Then my earlier question stands, what do they have on you?"

Loria exhaled sharply and moved over to rearrange the pillows.

"It was a stormy night." Instead of directly answering the question, he began with a seemingly unrelated introduction. "A man named Samuel Pilcher had been expecting a visit. Good old Sammy the Dodge." Loria paused to see if Wade was confused enough yet, then elaborated. "He had a nasty habit of dispatching his competitors by dragging them behind his Dodge truck, the only make he'd ever drive. American-made."

"How patriotic," Wade noted patiently.

"Yeah." Loria seemed to be heading for a self-induced trance.

His eyes circled the room – the heavy drapes, the penumbrae, the dim standard lamps – then froze, fixed in one direction.

"Everyone has their bleeding heart story. Mine wasn't anything extraordinary. Poor rich kid, agonizing teenage inadequacy, aggravated by a yet undiagnosed string of social disorders. I discovered heroin as a way of dealing with my problems, and it worked for a while. Until that night when the determination to get clean faded once again, and I felt myself going into withdrawal. Until that rainy night when cutting corners seemed a sport. I knew I hit something. I didn't find out what it was till the morning after, till the papers came. Dashaun

Williams, a devoted husband and a father of two, walking home after a late shift at Lou's, a nightclub where he worked as a janitor. I didn't even touch the brakes," Loria halted, staring into nothing.

"That was almost a year ago. And getting back to your earlier accusations, no, I didn't hire anybody to blackmail me. I'm not as insane as I apparently appear to be. And once again, no, I've never heard of Jessica whats-her-name. But there is a possible explanation I can offer for the brazen behavior you witnessed and for the insufficient amount of money asked."

"I'm listening," Wade waited.

"Today was not the first time I've paid up. And I'm sorry I didn't tell Tieri everything." Loria's eyes resumed their movement.

"Far from being the first demand, it's been going on for months now. I should've turned to the authorities earlier, I know. But call it what you will, repentance?" Loria uttered the rest in a rushed undertone. "If it weren't for those letters and the phone calls remorse wouldn't be sending me on the healing path now."

CHAPTER XXVI

Once again Aya had no control over the elevator's descent. She looked at the badge she'd appropriated from the shipment clerk who now laid stripped, securely tied and gagged, along with Phillip, the delivery driver, inside the intermediate underground chamber.

She felt uncomfortably hot in the borrowed uniform, but, on the other hand, she was glad the internal rules and regulations seemed to require standardized headgear. Aya tucked her hair in and pulled the cap over her face, certain she'd have to dodge a few cameras.

After what felt like forever the elevator door opened into an immaculate steel and glass corridor, and a wave of icy air blasted at Aya's body.

The cold was a typical wasteful practice of all gargantuan government and corporate structures that seemed dead set against conservationism. Or were the arctic temperatures simply directed at increasing productivity by keeping employees awake and alert?

Either way, the corridor ahead was employee-free for the time being and, with her head held low, Aya stepped out of the elevator.

The heels of her sandals gave off a sharp sound against the non-skid alloy floor, and she hoped the overhead camera wouldn't catch her bare toes peeking out of the bottom of her ill-fitting slacks.

As she proceeded, the walls on each side of the corridor interchangeably opened up into full-length oblong windows, the small chambers beyond bereft of human presence as well. Only a disarray of paperwork inside the cubicles gave them a lived-in feel.

Aya continued walking.

The corridor abruptly swerved and dead-ended with another elevator. Aya sized up the electronic control panel beside it and decided to turn back and try a few doors along the way.

For the camera's sake she performed a game of 'oh my god, I left my valuables behind' and took her best shot at picking a door that looked least like an entrance to an office full of cubicles.

Not that there was anything wrong with the offices. Aya was fairly sure the untidy stacks of paperwork and the desktop personal computers held some gems of information. But then again it was after hours, which meant those offices would most certainly be locked, and Aya didn't want to give herself away by not seeming to know her way around. At least not just yet.

She stopped herself from swearing aloud and once more wished she hadn't rendered the shipment clerk unconscious before asking a few questions.

A sturdy metal door just around the corner appeared to be different from the rest. Aya pushed the handlebar and miraculously it offered no resistance.

The door led to the top of a dimly lit stairwell. With no cameras in sight, Aya could afford to shrug off some of her nervous tension. Yet her mind kept racing a hundred miles per second, going back to the convenience store clerk upstairs, wondering how long she had till he became suspicious of Phillip's absence.

Two flights down, the stairs ended with another metal door. Aya groaned in disappointment at finding it bolted shut from the inside. Another dead end.

She paced the landing back and forth like a caged tiger.

What now? she asked herself. Should she go back upstairs, try an office and hope no one was keeping an eye on those surveillance tapes? Should she give up? Or maybe, if she were to get lucky, just maybe....

Aya looked up in search of an access point to the ventilation shaft. She saw a utility panel on the ceiling above her head and prayed it was not the day the maintenance crew purged the system.

She climbed onto the handrail to examine the bolts that held the panel in place, and a couple of good whacks with the butt of her gun later, pulled herself up into the narrow duct opening.

It was dark inside. A little too dark, considering the panel was still open.

Aya felt her way around. A surge of claustrophobia lapped at her stomach, as she realized the shaft was too narrow for her to turn around. Unless she came upon some roomier extensions along the way, she would have to crawl backwards on her return journey.

Aya took a deep breath of cold air and pushed on ahead.

Around the first bend, she heard a distant wheezing and hum, as a compressor came on to launch the fans spinning. Aya shielded her eyes against the initial gust and tasted grit between her teeth.

She crept on, making the slowest progress imaginable, until finally there was light. There was a vent up ahead and Aya held her breath, wondering what she would see when her eyes adjusted to the change.

What she saw was just another room, as blindingly white as the rest of them. Aya brought her face closer to the steel grating of the vent, but all she could make out from her vantage point was a glass wall.

Aya shifted her body to see what was behind it, but the obstacle turned out to be not a wall at all, but a large glass container. There were air tubes connected to its side, a giant lung working its way up and down. Multi-colored hoses, the purpose of which Aya could only guess. And then, behind that tangled rubber mass, Aya saw a woman. Or rather a young girl. She couldn't be more than sixteen or seventeen. She sat inside the tank, crouched like a dog, with her arms hanging between her legs.

The girl was absolutely naked, though, for some strange reason, the fact didn't seem to bother her in any way. Neither did squatting on the glass floor. Her face expressed no seeming concern with her surroundings.

Before Aya could make heads or tails of what exactly she was witnessing, she heard a sudden bang from a door from below. A man in white overalls walked into the room, picked up a clipboard off the desk in the corner, then turned around to leave. He appeared entirely unconcerned with the contents of the glass chamber. The whole scene was utterly bizarre.

As her mind was slowly coming out of its dumb stupor, Aya felt that her arm had gone completely numb from the lack of movement. She tried to re-adjust her position, careful not to make any noise, when she could've sworn the girl heard her.

Her pupils moved in Aya's direction with a thoughtless, vacant stare.

Aya didn't understand right away what her own eyes were seeing, but as the girl's whole body turned to face the vent, Aya realized the thing she was looking at was not a girl at all. The way it leapt across its cage, was it even human? Aya saw the other side of its face and gasped....

CHAPTER XXVII

Unable to turn around within the confined quarters of the ventilation shaft, Aya took a moment to collect her thoughts. The creature in the room below seemed to have lost interest in her presence just as quickly as it had become aware of the intrusion in the first place. Aya weighed her alternatives and, instead of setting out on her way back through the shaft feet-first, decided to press on a little further ahead.

The next vent down the line opened into another white room. Much smaller in size than the first one, it contained a computer desk, a tall file cabinet and a glass door that apparently led into the room Aya had come across earlier.

The man in overalls who she had seen next door a minute ago sat in front of a desktop computer, his clipboard hanging on the wall next to the monitor. He was enjoying a game of Tetris. Company dollars hard at work, Aya noted.

She waited, trying to decide what she should do next, when the man suddenly got off his chair and walked out of the room. She heard another door bang shut in the distance.

Without wasting a second, Aya hooked her fingers on the vent's grating and lifted the cover out of the way. She stuck her head down to check for cameras. There were none in sight, but Aya pulled her cap closer over her eyes just the same and placed her knees above the vent opening.

The ceiling wasn't high and Aya lowered herself through with ease. The heels of her sandals connected with the rubber floor, and she took a step toward the desk. One step was all it took; the room proved even smaller than it had initially appeared.

Aya gave the glass door an apprehensive look to make sure there were no other employees around and reached for the clipboard on the wall. She saw the current date stamped at the top of the page and skimmed through the handwritten notes below.

'Lot Nineteen,' said the one and only entry, followed by a long string of medical read-outs. 'No further regression apparent. Metastatic tumor lesions completely rejected.'

Aya replaced the clipboard to its original position and turned toward the computer screen. She minimized the Tetris window and scrutinized the desktop icons. The shortcut to the user documents looked promising and Aya moved the mouse over to open the reports folder inside. She then enabled the search function and scanned the contents for any data on Lot Nineteen. Before the search could retrieve all the results, she double-clicked the first file.

'A. Wallace,' said the box at the top of the screen. 'Stage 4S neuroblastoma with dissemination to liver and bone marrow. External damage to upper extremities. Electrofusion produced a hybrid of autologous tumor and allogeneic dendritic cells that presented antigens expressed by the tumor in concert with the co-stimulating capabilities of dendritic cells.'

Too pressed for time to try and decipher the heavy terminology before her, Aya moved on to the next file.

'November 12, 2003', it stated and continued on in short bursts of information. 'Hybrid antigen administered successfully. Cell regeneration response mixed. Axolotl string dominant.'

Axolotl, Aya paused to grasp at the meaning of the word. Wasn't it something that had to do with a... Before Aya could complete her thought, she heard the door in the next room open. She rushed to close out the files and jumped to pull herself back up though the vent opening.

What did it all mean? she wondered as she slid the vent cover carefully shut. Neuroblastoma was a type of cancer, but why would Neuetech go to such length to keep the existence of the New River lab a secret? A. Wallace, whoever that might be, was apparently dying of cancer, and Neuetech had saved that patient's life. If that was the case, then why hide the fact? Was the success not all Neuetech wanted it to be? And what did it have to do with the thing locked up inside that glass container anyway?

And then, as Aya was crawling back through the dark shaft toward the exit, she understood.

CHAPTER XVIII

Ronnie Halprin scooted over into the driver's seat and inserted the key back into ignition. He considered turning on the radio, but after a little thought decided against it, worried that even the slightest noise might attract unwanted attention. He could not afford to get in trouble. At least not more than he was in already.

Why was he here? How had he gotten himself into this situation? Sitting in his new car in the middle of the desert, covered with dust. If it had been up to him, he'd be home relaxing. But he wasn't. Aya had dragged him along on her crazy scheme instead. He sure hadn't volunteered.

For a second he felt almost angry. He thought of driving off, going home (Pinky must be really hungry by now), leaving Aya behind in the dust.

But, of course, he couldn't. He wouldn't. And not only because he prided himself on being a person of integrity, but because (and he felt goosebumps on the back of his neck just for thinking it) he was genuinely intrigued by the ways of the

125

criminal mind. Because the whole experience of meeting Aya Morell and assisting the course of justice seemed like something out of a TV show, something of that once-in-a-lifetime quality, and he was lucky that she let him play along.

So there he was, sitting alone in his car in the middle of the desert. And he would stay there as long as he had to. He was the lucky one.

***

Outside it was getting dark. Ronnie could see the perimeter lights of the gas station come on. The front windows lit up.

The semi remained parked. Ronnie began to worry. He wondered how much time had passed since Aya had left. He really wished he had looked at his watch. How long had she been gone? An hour? Longer? Should he go and see what was going on? Aya might need help.

She had said for him to leave if she wasn't back after a couple of hours. How could he not have looked at his watch? He really should have paid better attention.

Tension getting the best of him, Ronnie was about to get out of the car when a loud pop ripped through the night air.

Backfire? Ronnie wondered. Unlikely. That semi wouldn't be still running, would it? Why was it still there anyway?

Something must've happened.

Ronnie flung the door open and jumped out of the car. He wasn't sure what it was he was about to do. All he could think of was to try and make that damn automatic interior light go off. Ronnie struggled with the switch, too anxious for the idea of shutting the door to occur to him.

He was interrupted by the sound of running footsteps. Before he had time to react he heard Aya's voice.

"Drive! Drive!" she said urgently.

He flopped back into the driver's seat and turned the ignition, tires screeching as he tore out of the hiding place.

Aya exhaled with exhaustion beside him. She didn't seem to be hurt. At least not seriously enough to show bloodstains.

"What is it? What happened? What did you see?" Ronnie balanced out the steering.

The gas pumps and the semi's running lights disappeared within the rear-view mirror.

CHAPTER XXIX

Over the hum of the engine Ronnie heard her laugh.

"What?" Puzzled, he took his eyes off the road to make sure she wasn't crying hysterically instead. He could never tell with women. "What's so funny?"

"Nothing, nothing." Choking with laughter, Aya shook her head to brush off an involuntary tear.

"Nothing?" Ronnie's enthusiasm veered off into the unease he so often felt of late. "I heard a gunshot. I think. Was it a gunshot? I swear…"

"Ronnie," she didn't let him finish. "Thank you for being here tonight. And don't worry, I was careful. There'll be no slugs to pick out."

"No slugs?" Ronnie coughed, once again glancing in Aya's direction.

She looks different, he thought.

"That place is more than meets the eye, I'll tell you that much," she went on. "Unfortunately I didn't have enough time to get far."

There was something wild in her eyes. Was she even the same person? But, of course, she was; how could she not be?

Ronnie fidgeted and concentrated on the road.

"Guns are overrated, Ronnie," he heard her drawl. "One shouldn't depend on guns alone. Nevertheless, they are a thing of beauty. An object d'art, wouldn't you say?"

She didn't wait for him to agree.

"They are intimidating to some people, that's a large part of their power. But to actually pull the trigger, to intend for the bullet to hit more than empty space; that's special."

From the corner of his eye Ronnie saw her pick up a black pistol, flip it from one hand to the other.

"One of the guards let me borrow this. Do you know what it is?"

"Careful with that!" Ronnie couldn't hold back a nervous warning.

"Walther P99 quick action. Ambidextrous magazine release. Quite popular with police tactical units." Without missing a beat, her tone suddenly turned grave. "I like you, Ronnie. You are, however misguided, however overprotective of yourself, a sweet person at heart."

A nice thing to say, but why was she saying it? What had happened to her at that gas station?

"Would you mind if we switched seats?" Aya's words were suddenly icy.

CHAPTER XXX

Statewide. Non-profit.

Central New Mexico Correctional Facility at Los Lunas.

Male and female inmates of all security levels.

The nondescript monochrome of a warehouse-like structure slumbered ahead, as Wade pulled up to the guard booth and rolled down his window.

"Gavin Wade," he said to the uniform on duty and passed his ID badge for verification. "I'm expected."

The guard reached over to take a good look at Wade's badge and with a "Just a minute, sir" turned away to check the daily visitation sheets. He then gave a satisfied nod and pushed the gate release.

"Drive on in, sir," the guard said. "You can park in the visitor's zone straight ahead, then go through the main entrance and check in at the information booth inside."

"Thank you." Wade rolled his window back up and pulled through the now open gate into the long driveway ahead.

Once inside the building, Wade identified himself to the

guard on the other side of the shatterproof glass window in the foyer.

"I'm here to see inmate Samuel Pilcher," he announced.

The guard glanced at Wade's badge, then reached to turn down the volume on a portable television sitting beside his PC monitor.

"Do you have an appointment, sir?"

"I called yesterday," Wade gave a curt nod.

The guard popped a keyboard out from under his desk, his fingers hammering away at the keys.

"Pilcher? That's P-i-l-c-h-e-r?" He double-checked the spelling.

"Samuel," Wade confirmed.

"This might take a few minutes." The guard's rolling chair slid closer to the intercom. "Why don't you take a seat?"

A foyer? A waiting room? A serpent's head. Whatever the premises were, they looked hardly wider than the rest of the narrow hallway that tailed beyond.

Wade sat down on something that bore a strong resemblance to a lawn chair and waited.

Tick-tock, a Quartz clock on the gray cement wall above the entrance doors. Tick-tock, echoing through the empty corridors, over the cheap linoleum floor tiles, basking in the harsh fluorescent lighting.

The rhythmic two-tone was abruptly overpowered by the sound of the newscast coming from the TV set inside the guard's booth. A female voice, delivering the lines with intense determination.

"A body of a John Doe has been found here, dumped on the side of Highway 66 West near Defiance, approximately seven miles from the Arizona border. According to the police statement, the victim is a Caucasian male in his early forties, five foot seven, weighing a hundred and ninety pounds. He has brown eyes and light-brown thinning hair and was wearing blue jeans and a plain white T-shirt. Preliminary reports state a single gunshot wound to the head as the cause of death. No form of identification or any personal effects were found, except for this two-by-three inch laminated photo stuck in the back pocket of the victim's jeans. You can see it on your screen now. The photo shows John Doe sitting on a couch next to a Hispanic-looking young woman, possibly his wife or a girlfriend, with a ginger-colored cat in his lap. If you have any information related to the crime and the victim's identity, or if you recognize the woman in the photo, please contact your local police department as soon as possible. I'm Diana Kelley for KASA Fox 2 news, Albuquerque. Back to you, Ned."

Whatever comments Ned had to make were cut short, drowned out by the buzzing intercom.

CHAPTER XXXI

Wade took the mug shot print out of his pocket and unfolded it in front of the man in orange prison overalls waiting on the opposite side of the safety glass wall.

Another lovely green plastic lawn chair, Wade noted sitting down. Where's the barbecue grill anyway? Bound to be tucked away in one of these corners. Garden Ridge must have had a blowout sale the week the prison got furnished.

Wade pulled the receiver off the hook and watched the other man repeat the action.

A big guy, that one, tall enough to have to lean forward to rest his elbows on the counter. His immoderately developed biceps bulged out from under the short sleeves of his prison uniform. His flaring nostrils did not look likely to entail a sweet disposition. All in all, Samuel Pilcher would hardly need a Dodge to trample a man over.

"Looks familiar?" Skipping formalities, Wade jumped straight to the subject of the printout.

"Whoa, whoa, whoa...." Pilcher protested in a soothing baritone that didn't quite go with his wrestler physique. "What's the rush? Don't got a minute to say hello to a brother?"

Wade made an assertive motion, pointing first to himself, then toward his interlocutor. "Gavin Wade. Sammy the Dodge. Nice to finally meet you."

"That be me, baby. Although that particular name is members only. Reserved for friends and family. Are you a friend?" Pilcher clamped the receiver between his broad shoulder and whatever neck he had and criss-crossed his fingers in his doomsday prophet moment.

"I'm here to help you," Wade felt the time to repent was as good as any. "So I guess you can say I'm a friend, yeah."

Pilcher puffed the air out of his nostrils. "Help me, huh? So how is it your questions are gonna help *me*?"

"Rumors are going around, Sammy," Wade shrugged. "They say your appeal is in trouble."

"You been misinformed, baby," Pilcher's log-sized index finger flew up righteously. "Ain't nothing wrong with my appeal."

"Not what I've heard," Wade walked a fine line between confidence and mockery, but then again, playing audacious was a lot easier from his side of the glass wall. "I've heard your woman sold you out. Promised you a nice vacation, dry climate, clean air. A week later called the cops on you. Abduction, not a desirable addition to your already colorful resume. But, I'll say, you did get that vacation, dry climate and all."

Wade saw Pilcher's upper lip twitch, just before the receiver boomed close to blowing the circuit.

"That charge is all lies, and you know it! The bitch is nothing but a liar. Everyone knows. The judge knows. They only convicted me in the first place 'cos they don't have nothing else on me. Clean, baby. Clean as a whistle!" Pilcher clenched his substantial fists, as if ready to squash any obstacle on the way to his upcoming freedom.

"Glad to hear that," Wade continued, ignoring Pilcher's riveting showcase of a wasted stage talent. "There's only this one thing, but you won't be interested in hearing it then." Wade made an over dramatized attempt to get up.

"I ain't begging if that's what you expect," Pilcher tilted back, his chair on the verge of snapping to pieces.

"Fine, I'll tell it to you anyway." Wade flopped back down, as if unable to contain the news. "Remember that assault on Judge Stegman a few months ago? She announced her intention to retire shortly after it happened. Ring any bells? Well, she's still retiring, but not before she handles one last case." Wade slipped in a meaningful pause. "Guess whose?"

"Oh shit!" Pilcher let the receiver out of his shoulder cradle, only to catch it with both his hands and bang it hard against the counter.

"I wonder why she's being so particular," Wade's unaffected voice picked up just where it left off when Pilcher found himself fit enough to listen again. "Perhaps someone told her something about that assault."

"Who would..." Pilcher screwed up his face. "You? How? You know I had nothing to do with that. I'm a nice guy. I don't play games like that."

"Are you sure? Because I could ask around."

Pilcher bottom lip trembled, "You're bullshitting me, right?"

Wade only raised his eyebrows in an attempt at ambiguity.

"Motherfucker!" Pilcher swore, proceeding to declare his firm intent to sue for unethical police procedure if anyone at all interfered with his appeal, then reversed his tactics and threw out the white flag instead.

"Let's see that damn picture again," he grumbled.

Wade didn't need a second invitation. "Jessica Ann Katz, know her?" He held the printout up once more.

"Yeah, I know her," Pilcher said, victimized. "No loyalties there. Used to go by Vivian then, but I'm sure there's more false ID's in that girl's purse than shoes in her closet. And she loved shoes, believe me. Bitches are crazy 'bout shoes. But that one," he shook his head while stealing the last, almost tender, glance at the print. "A real artist that one, a hard worker."

"What's that supposed to mean?"

"She likes to get into your head," Pilcher put his finger up to his temple in a drill-like motion. "She watches you, writes it all down in her little black book, studies your weaknesses, then plays a goddamned aria on them."

"Who is she working for?" Wade leaned forward in anticipation.

Pilcher shrugged it off. "Bitch got issues with authority, trusts no one. Everyone else in their right mind wouldn't trust her enough to work with her either."

"Where does she get her information?"

"Buys it off the street, twists it and turns it until those poor schmucks don't know the truth themselves. Then she bleeds them dry, drop by drop. 'You can drain a sucker for lots more, if you don't get too greedy too fast,' she used to say. If you ask what business she's in, she'll say, 'Finance. Where good things come in small installments.'"

"A former client of yours, Leonard Loria, did you sell him to her?"

"So she got to him, huh?" Pilcher chuckled, pleased. "Not even gonna ask what piece she used. Dude's a creep."

"Gloating alone is not too helpful to me, Sammy," Wade cut him short. "Come on, try harder, put your mind to it, brighten up my day."

"Try Eddie Bell," Pilcher said after a moment of deliberation. "He owns a fish market in Jersey City. Tuesday is his busy day. That's all I got for you."

Wade was halfway across the room before he heard pounding on the glass and ran back to grab the receiver before the guard had a chance to drag Pilcher off.

"Yo, FBI," said the velvet voice in Wade's ear. "Here's another motherfucking gesture of good will toward mankind for you. Whatever you do, don't get your cop ass inside the place. Eddie's got a nose for fuzz, he'll spot you like that."

Pilcher snapped his fingers soundlessly before being escorted away.

CHAPTER XXXII

New York City.

Aya took in a breath of the smog and noise pollution of the early morning rush hour, then quickly shut the window.

A fancy room in a posh hotel. A company credit card in her pocketbook. A splitting headache.

Why was she here?

Aya clutched at her temples, trying to squeeze away the pain.

What had brought her here? Was it by her own will? Why couldn't she remember?

Questions came and went without answers. The headache was now shaping itself into nausea.

Aya ran for the restroom.

Was she hung over? Surely not. It had been two days since the tequilas with Ronnie, and she hadn't had a drink since then. Or had she?

A splash of cold water made Aya's skin tingle. Her wet fingers ran through her hair, over the fresh stubble around the stitches. Perhaps she had overestimated the speed of her recovery, and she wasn't such a fast healer after all.

Aya rinsed out her mouth and buried her face in a fuzzy towel hoping for fuzzy feelings to follow.

What was she forgetting?

Last night's confusion? The midnight flight out of Phoenix? Maltais' voice, vaguely excited, on the other end of the line.

"I do hope your injury is better, I need you to say that New York sounds great."

"New York?" Aya's own voice echoing. "What's in New York?"

"Oishi. He contacted us an hour ago, willing to negotiate his terms."

"What does he want?"

"That," Maltais sucked in air noisily, before carrying on, "you are to find out. He only requested our agent to be checked into the Wellington by tomorrow morning and wait for his call. You're up for it?"

"Wires?" she asked.

"No, we were discretely advised against that. We will, however, get someone in to watch your back. Just in case things get..."

Aya almost heard him say 'hairy', but at the last moment Maltais decided to stay true to his usual monochrome demeanor.

"In case things go wrong," he concluded. "I'm telling you this so if you happen to spot a shadow, it's not anything to worry about."

"Why me?" A perfect final question.

Yes, why send her? She had let Oishi get away once already. She'd been clumsy enough; can a woman do anything right?

She remembered Maltais' answer now, as she lay on the hotel bed, staring aimlessly at the ceiling. The answer that had nothing to do with her being inferior in any of Maltais' chauvinistic ways. Nor did it have to do with her being expendable. And what's more important, it didn't even paint her as an unwanted threat to be eliminated, the one who's spying while hunting for a spy.

The answer had nothing to do with her crimes and virtues, yet everything to do with her. The four words she did not expect to hear.

"He asked for you."

CHAPTER XXXIII

Grabbing a nap proved most refreshing. More so after a sleepless night between airports.

Not that Aya was afraid of flying. It was not the height that kept her restless, but the sense of constant motion. Perhaps her mother never rocked her off to sleep, never cared enough for infants to hold Aya in her arms. Or at least that's what Freud would have assumed.

That was not to say that her mother wasn't there for Aya in times of need. She had been. Her mother always had been there to sort out Aya's teenage messes, to keep up a good appearance with all the devotion she could muster. If only she had also given Aya her understanding and approval.

Oh, she had loved her daughter all right; she had loved her ghost of a husband and the husband before him. She just didn't love them in a way that would make anyone happy.

But that was all so long ago. Why was Aya thinking of it now? She had hardly even spoken to her parents in years. An occasional phone call, just to let them know she was still alive. A

141

postcard now and then. No blow-ups. No blame and accusations. Not after the fact had finally sunk in. Their little girl, their only child would never become what they had hoped for, would not pay dues to family traditions.

And in the end, distance was all that they had left. An insurmountable void. And neither needed the other anymore.

***

Aya forced the unwelcome memory out of her mind and slid off the bed.

A fresh set of clothes, a stroke of a hairbrush and a touch of lip-gloss later she was awake at last, with a surprisingly strong craving for caffeine.

She considered going downstairs for a cup of coffee, possibly to have a look around, but would she be the only one to do the looking?

Aya remembered Maltais' promise to have someone to watch her back and wondered if the shadow man was already in place. Had he been waiting for her to get off the plane, watching her hail a cab, carry her suitcase across the hotel lobby? Was he still there now? Sitting on a couch, pretending to be reading yesterday's paper?

How long would it take her to spot him? How easily could she shake him off?

No, she should probably stay in her room instead, order in, wait for Oishi's call.

Aya sat back down on the bed to take off her shoes, when the vibration of her cell gave her a sudden jolt.

"Morell." She flipped the phone open.

"I'm glad you made it." Aya recognized the voice at once, though this time it was not pleading, no longer hesitant. "Our prior encounter wasn't under the best of circumstances." A voice of a man on top of his game, cherishing his re-established control. "Though the real question is, are you here, to seek my apprehension, or the answers I could give you?"

Aya had no time for head games. "Where are you?" She pulled the straps of her sandals back around her ankles.

"Da Silvano's, a charming little sidewalk place on 6th. Be there in half an hour."

He paused, then added in a half-whisper as only a conspirator would. "I would say 'come alone', but I'm fairly positive you will be."

IRYNA BENNETT

CHAPTER XXXIV

Before its scheduled time, a lone streetlight flickered on to chase the harsh late afternoon shadows off the weathered sign mounted over a gateless gap in a rusted chain link fence. Eddie's fish market was a dark, dilapidated barn-like structure at the end of the driveway. It seemed to be deserted, except for the northerly wind playing tag with a mangled newspaper page.

Wade let his head fall into his hands and rubbed his face vigorously, trying to keep awake. His senses rushed back to him with the smell of seawater and a distant sound of screeching automobile brakes.

He looked up to catch sight of a black Audi speeding toward the service entrance of the market and disappearing into the back parking lot. Maybe something. Probably nothing. Vehicles of all shapes and sizes had been driving up to the place since dawn, but he'd seen no hint of Jessica's presence so far.

Wade waited a minute before starting his car, then took off the parking brake and circled the block.

The change of location brought into view the delivery gate

enclosed by a row of industrial garbage collection bins. Wade killed the engine and, binoculars on stand-by, leaned back in his seat to stretch.

The remains of the daylight were slowly forsaking the desolate streets, the vacant pier, the wilted shrubbery by the roadside. A feeling of hunger replaced Wade's idle drowsiness.

It *was* Tuesday, wasn't it? He *had* been staking the place out all day, just like Pilcher told him to, hadn't he? Watching people come and go, boats dock and drift away, trucks being loaded and unloaded, the previously faint, raw fish odor growing more nauseating with each tick of the dashboard clock.

8:15: Wade's stomach turned, insisting that a man could not be sustained by pre-dawn breakfast alone.

8:16: Wade's brain interfered to suggest it was no time to think about food.

8:17: Stomach begged to differ.

8:18: Severe doubts about the entire affair entered Wade's mind and refused to leave. The owner of the Audi, just like others before him and more to follow, would certainly end up being nothing but another employee, going about whatever employee business there was to attend to. Sammy Pilcher had made it all up— Tuesdays, fish markets, the whole shebang— just to get the badge off his back. Wade could not believe he had been idiot enough to even consider taking Pilcher's advice at face value.

8:19: The further battle of spirit and flesh was interrupted by the motion of the barn's heavy service door sliding open.

A half-second later Wade flung the binoculars up to his eyes. Unmistakable. Unquestionable. Not even to be hoped for. Jessica Ann Katz, and none other, slipped out of the building and into the dusk of the Audi's interior.

His mind suddenly clear, Wade restarted the engine and, carefully keeping at a safe distance, pulled out in pursuit, southbound to the New Jersey turnpike.

CHAPTER XXXV

Rows of cozy, gated communities sprung up like poison weeds on either side of the road. Arborlane, Arborlawn, Arborview. Cookie cutter stone-slab nameplates drifted through Wade's peripheral vision as he eased off the gas pedal to let the Audi pull through one of the automated entrance gates.

He then left his car parked by the curb and moved silently to a spot away from the brightest streetlights where he jumped the split rail fencing.

Wade intentionally misread the private property posting as he, in a seemingly aimless fashion, wandered the streets among the gingerbread facades of the town homes, the dimly lit shallow ponds, the excess of artfully pruned shrubbery, and those necessary evils of architecture, the carports.

When he finally spotted the Audi, Wade knelt down beside its badly dented quarter panel to make out the space number painted on the asphalt in the corner of the parking spot, the shadow of the carport compressing the darkness even more densely.

Wade deciphered the number, 32B, and hoped the object of his pursuit respected the rules of reserved parking.

With the information acquired from the faded paint he carefully approached the front lawn of unit 32B and, avoiding the mist from a pixie fountain, halted by the ivy-enshrouded brick wall.

The porch light was on. The living-room window, however, displayed no sign of indoor activity.

Keeping close to the ivy, Wade proceeded around the building to find the narrow kitchen window lit, muffled voices carrying from within.

Wade listened. Unable to hear enough to figure out the content of the conversation, he pulled himself up the window ledge and peeked inside through the veil of a semi-transparent curtain.

A man and a woman in the middle of a blindingly immaculate floor. Wade was almost positive that they had been arguing over something a minute ago, but now they were silent. The woman only stood there, loosening the ponytails of her long black hair, setting it free into the sparkling white of the room.

Her hair slithered with a life of its own down her bare shoulders, obliterating from view the spaghetti straps of her ivory camisole, creeping across the snow of the man's cotton shirt.

Jessica Ann Katz. Neither their previous meeting downtown, with all her excessively loud attire, nor the blurry, less than excellent quality of the mug shot printout gave justice to the china-doll fragility of her beauty.

She *was* beautiful. Breathtakingly, exquisitely beautiful when stripped of all her practiced defenses.

Had there been a curse cast over him, Wade wondered, a punishment of some sort, always having to face unattainable perfection? Coincidence? Or dissatisfaction with his own ordinary existence that caused him to strive for an unreachable mark?

Wade had no answers; he only watched Jessica's sensuous lips brush up against her companion's in a cold, detached manner. She whispered in the man's ear, and then both figures disappeared into the darkness of the hallway beyond.

CHAPTER XXXVI

Wade slept in the car. Or rather spent the night in the car, since sitting up with your eyes barely shut for fear of the suspect legging it again hardly qualified as sleeping. His back muscles felt sore from the lack of movement, his legs numb. His empty stomach was past caring.

He was about to come out of the car and stretch when the gate to the townhouse community slid open and the first of its inhabitants began leaving to get an early jump on their workday. Jessica Ann proved an early bird herself, whatever busy schedule she had awaiting her attentions. No longer in the company of the man Wade had seen her with the previous night, she pulled through the gate and headed out, back in the direction of the Jersey turnpike.

The morning sun found Wade in the parking lot of the Newport pier. He left his rental car a few spaces behind Jessica's Audi and followed her inside the pier building. He bought a packaged cinnamon roll from a vending machine in the lobby and devoured it, too tired to fantasize about the breakfast in bed he could have had if he had spent the night in the comfort of Loria Inn. He was even too tired to blame Tieri for the evaporated prospects of quiet relaxation and reflection, for that growing feeling of being duped.

Out of all Loria's prior unfounded paranoias, why was it this one that had to be proven real? Why had Wade agreed to take the case in the first place, when he was ready to resign from his job? Was he that easily swayed? Or were his intentions not distinct enough to prove him anything but gullible?

Wade blinked away a surge of anxiety and inhaled the morning breeze as he stepped aboard the ferry.

He would deal with the consequences one at a time, Wade attempted to rationalize. In spite of his seeming indecision, it was after all entirely up to him to quit any time he wished. The real question was whether he really wanted to.

Wade looked away from the murky waters disrupted by the ferry's keel and returned his gaze toward Jessica Ann's slender figure leaning over the sideboard rail. Toward the denim jacket she wore over her white top. The perfect crows of her flyaway hair.

And all of a sudden disgust flooded over him with an unexpected force. And Wade knew. The answer to his earlier questions presented itself clear as day, a path away from the criminal field calling out with its carefree lack of obligation.

There would be no more swaying, no more being seduced by perfection. For he realized, were his hand to touch that otherworldly beauty by the sideboard rail, her skin would feel scaly and cold, like that of a viper.

Would Aya's skin feel the same way if he ever dared to come close enough to find out?

Disgust and pity flooded over Wade only to be pushed away toward the back of his mind by the ferry's horn.

Peer 11 awaited. Along with its procession of omnipresent taxis.

CHAPTER XXXVII

She must've had an appointment to keep. When they reached West 16th, Jessica paid her cabby and went inside a modest-looking cafe with a glass façade.

Wade found himself a window seat in the one across the street and hoped that whoever she was waiting for wouldn't be along just yet. He ordered a coffee and a club sandwich and felt composure for the first time in a long while.

Perhaps it was only the caffeine talking, but maybe, just maybe, he was finally on his way. To somewhere, anywhere. Away from this. A plan was finally forming in his head.

He would stick with this case until it was closed, as promised. And then....

He looked through the window across the street and saw Jessica order another drink. She took a small sip, then slipped off her stool and headed toward the bar.

"Sir," at first Wade didn't realize the waitress was addressing him. "You have a phone call."

"Me?" Baffled by the idea of anyone knowing of his

whereabouts, Wade settled the check and, still keeping an eye on the café across the street, approached the counter.

"Hello," he said, hesitantly, upon accepting the receiver.

"You have been following me," a harsh female voice at the other end of the line.

Wade switched hands nervously, yet the tension did not reflect in his voice. "One should expect that in your line of work, Jessica."

"No one calls me that." He heard her exhale. "You're Loria's lapdog, aren't you? Don't think you're the only one who does his homework. I recognized you for what you are the minute I laid eyes on your cop face at the money drop the other day. I have a way with people, you see. I saw right through you. And then today on the ferry. The location couldn't have been more perfect to try and arrest me. So why didn't you? Can't swim?"

She was laughing. An impish little laugh. Taunting and cruel.

"Give it up, Jessica." Wade was too exhausted to nurture injured pride, his mind working through all the possible ways Jessica could have planned for her escape. "My client doesn't want a public display, even if it's your arrest we're talking about. Whatever you have on him, just give it up."

"I already have, you dumb pig," came another disdainful answer. "My technique does not include dealing with the likes of you. The pond is filled with better fish. Go home. Tell your boy it's over, because you won't be lucky enough to find me again."

She hung up and was gone from the window. Wade dropped the receiver back on its cradle and ran out into the street. A single thought, accompanied by nothing but pure relief, rushed through his head as he pushed through the door of the café that had allowed Jessica her getaway. Almost over, almost over.

"A girl, dark hair, denim jacket," he flashed his badge at the wait staff.

Someone pointed to the rear exit.

Almost over.

CHAPTER XXXVIII

There was no trace of Jessica in the side alley or in the street beyond. For the sake of being methodical Wade combed through the empty restrooms and the kitchen of the café before calling it quits. He walked a block toward 10th Avenue and hailed a cab.

"Loria Inn," he said to the driver.

It was all finally over, and Loria could do whatever his heart desired with the information Wade had gathered. Loria could file official charges against his blackmailer. Or he could deal with her in his own twisted way. Wade no longer cared.

The cab was almost at the steps of Loria Inn when Wade suddenly realized there was a loose end left. The man Jessica had spent the night with in Jersey City, who was he? Was he in on the extortion scheme or simply an innocent bystander? Jessica's personal friend?

"Turn around," Wade called out to the cabby. "Take me to Jersey City."

He had to know this one last thing.

The cab raced through Holland tunnel, reaching its

destination in time for Wade to witness the man in question leave the luxuries of the townhouse community and catch a cab to Manhattan.

At the corner of 55th, the pursued vehicle pulled over to the curb and waited, while its passenger went inside a hotel foyer, only to return ten minutes later. The car then pulled back onto 7th Street and made another stop just past King Street. The passenger exited and, with his jacket folded over his arm, joined the pedestrian flow northward.

Eyes locked in on the dark pinstripe shirt in the crowd ahead, Wade paid his own cabby and followed his prey, slowing his pace, as the man in question turned into a corner shop.

The suspect emerged minutes later, now wearing the jacket, and headed toward a café next door. He walked past the entrance and joined a young woman sitting with her back toward Wade at an outside table.

Her thin neck, the nonchalant pose, the contour of her leg in a high-heel shoe seemed suddenly all strangely too familiar, as the man leaned over to her ear, then got up to leave.

The woman hesitated, held her thought and then turned around to see her interlocutor off. As she did, a strand of her short blond hair fell, teased by the wind, across her face, while she blankly stared at Da Silvano's neon sign.

CHAPTER XXXIX

Aya didn't bother with change. Her stiletto scraped against hot asphalt, as she waved the cabby off and pulled up a chair at the corner table outside Da Silvano's.

She touched the gun at her thigh to reassure herself it was there and ordered a cappuccino to provide a necessary distraction (as well as the means of preventing caffeine withdrawal), then scanned the surrounding area.

The post-lunchtime hour found the old shopping stretch quietly relaxed, only the brick storefronts boasting a multitude of brightly colored insignia.

An odd number of slow-moving jaywalkers, a lanky graybeard hanging by a newsstand, a maroon Saturn parked across from a cigar place, a taxicab behind it. A light breeze meandered down the street, toying with Aya's hair, rustling in the leaves of a rosebush that sprawled lavishly just outside the shadow of Da Silvano's green overhang.

The question Oishi had asked her kept running through Aya's mind. "Are you here to seek my apprehension?"

Of course she wasn't planning to get Oishi arrested. At least not there, not then.

Then why had she come? Why did she come running like a dog drooling over a promise of a biscuit?

Was she simply following her employer's orders? Was she acting in the interest of the company? Had she ever been known to do that?

Not really. Though neither Maltais, nor anyone else could have known that just by looking at her glowing early retirement recommendations.

The truth was that the Bureau was only covering its rear, trying (and succeeding) to shut Aya up. The truth was she didn't give a rat's ass about Maltais or his damn company and all their hopes and wishes thrown together.

Then what? What kept her from getting up and walking away that very instant?

The shadow man? Curiosity? New River Road? Something else?

Something drawing her in and never letting go? What?

***

Aya's attempt at self-analysis was interrupted by Oishi's appearance. He walked out of the gift shop next door with his familiar, thin physique, his hands down in the pockets of his jacket, as if he were cold.

"A glass of Burgundy, please," Oishi excused the waiter and joined Aya at her table.

His fingertips landed on the edge of the heavy glass surface, the overly long sleeves of his dress shirt refusing to be hidden inside the jacket.

"Before you reach for that toy on your hip again, I should really warn you against any sudden moves," he said without hello and gave an apologetic half-smile. "Friends of mine are watching over my well-being."

"Dannii?" Aya presumed, resisting an immediate impulse to examine the storefronts.

"Perhaps," he said in a quiet baritone, his eyes staring into hers with... Was it curiosity?

"Your bodyguard?" Aya pushed the subject further. "Your lover?"

Oishi lowered his head, as if to shame her.

"I would like to see this conversation as a casual one." He pulled back, to make way for the waiter. "I'd like you to tell me why it is you're sitting here with a Beretta strapped under your skirt."

They *had* been watching her, whoever those friends of his were. However uncomfortable Aya found the idea of someone peeking through her windows, it didn't seem worth losing a staring match over.

"I'm here for the answers," Aya said, her voice unwavering.

"To take them back to Maltais?" His full upper lip caressed the red of the wine.

"To understand you," Aya persisted convincingly, yet Oishi's cynicism only flirted with the idea of being convinced.

"What's going down at New River Road?" Aya kept on. "What's on the disk?"

"Questions, questions. They would tire my mind." He set his glass down, without ever taking a sip. "I've made some inquiries about you. I imagine you've done your homework as well." He didn't wait for her to react. "My parents. I'd like them to be an immediate topic of this conversation."

"They died in a car wreck in 1985." What was he trying to get at?

"Not good enough." He clinked the stem of his glass against her cup and finished off his drink at one gulp. Then he leaned forward toward her ear, his hair prickly against her cheek.

"I wouldn't go back to your hotel room if I were you."

CHAPTER XL

Aya Morell.

Should he start to believe in fortune telling?

Some fifteen minutes ago, Wade would've sworn their paths would never cross again. And yet there she was, standing in the middle of the mid-afternoon street in one of her indecently short skirts, hailing a cab. She hadn't changed a bit.

What in the hell was she doing here in New York with that creep anyway? Wasn't her job contract at some place in sunny Arizona? Or did Aya's new employer not appreciate the subtleties of her professional etiquette either?

What was the nature of that little tête-à-tête Wade had just witnessed? Was Aya working an assignment, gathering information? What were the chances of her and Wade investigating the same case? Not particularly high, Wade would have presumed. More likely, close to nil.

Should he simply write off his running into Aya as a general coincidence, one of life's ironies? Or was she there plotting to somehow get back at the Bureau?

Whatever the case, she had some explaining to do, and Wade felt Aya could provide all the answers he ever needed.

Wade instructed his cabby to follow Aya's, his mind suddenly switching from the practical to the matters irrational, going back to the balmy barmaid-slash-card-reader and her fortune tales.

No, of course Wade didn't believe in all that extrasensory rubbish, the girl's every word was a mere charade – a fact not about to be altered. Why then did he wish he had been a little less drunk and a little more attentive that night? To disprove the predictions? How can you try and disprove something you don't believe was there in the first place?

What was it she had said? In spite of itself Wade's mind persisted.

Something about an untrustworthy, beautiful, dark woman. Should he assume that referred to Jessica Katz?

What else? Some babble about hidden dangers and the ten of wands. Wade was surprised that particular card stood out in his memory. A blonde, who was not who he thought she was. Wade did not dare make another assumption.

And what was that last card? But, of course, the barmaid never revealed its meaning, blaming herself for incompetence instead.

It was just a charade, Wade insisted to himself. It was nothing but a ruse, a sick little mind game. Why was he even entertaining the possibility of any of it being true?

Aya's taxi passed over the Manhattan Bridge and got off Flatbush Avenue at De Kalb.

Brooklyn Tech, is that where she was headed? What sort of a case would be bringing her there? Judging by the empty parking lot the faculty was gone for the summer. So who was she there to see?

Wade watched, as Aya knocked on the front door, stood there waiting, knocked once more, then walked aimlessly along the building's facade. Her visit was not expected after all. And as she disappeared behind the corner, Wade knew it was time to get to know his cabby a little better.

CHAPTER XLI

1985. Aya thought back to Oishi's file as she finished her cappuccino at Da Silvano's in solitude. Oishi had been fourteen then. A young talent, living in the suburbs, attending a school in the city. Of course, Aya finally realized where she should start her search for the answers upon which Oishi was so insistent. His old school.

She jumped out of her chair, suddenly inspired, and hailed a cab.

***

The modern day wonder found its humble beginnings in 1918 with a certain Dr. Albert L. Colston and his vision of scholastic grandeur.

Nearly nine decades later, there it was, Brooklyn Tech in all the glory of her academic and architectural supremacy. Waiting to inspire, to challenge. The sharp outline of her facade bearing down on the otherwise uneventful skyline.

Aya let the cab go and approached the formidable main entrance of the school to find doors made of solid steel bolted shut from the inside. These doors were made to keep something out. Or keep something in.

Aya knocked, or rather pounded, on the metal, took a step back and looked up.

Dense chain link covered the windows on the first two floors with flawless, impregnable symmetry.

Damn summer vacation, Aya realized. Of course, the doors would be locked; of course there would be no one inside.

Aya knocked once again, a purely habitual follow-up, and swore out loud at her own stupidity. She was definitely not dressed for rock climbing.

She walked the length of the sand-colored front wall toward the less dramatic structural addition at the south end of the complex. With a bit of luck, Aya hoped, a colossus such as this should have more than one way in. She prayed for a door with an actual lock she could pick.

To her considerable relief just around the corner Aya saw a green pick-up parked in the shade of a maple tree. Parked next to the back door of the school.

Bumblebee, Inc., said the sign across the truck's bed. What an odd name for a business, Aya thought. Unless, of course, honey was somehow involved. An unlikely prospect.

She circled around the vehicle and, finding no further indication as to what service its owner provided, approached the back entryway to the school.

Another steel frame. Aya exhaled, about to reapply her pounding technique, when she noticed the door was slightly ajar. Disregarding etiquette, she pulled the handle and slipped inside.

Whoever Fights Monsters

Penumbras reigned the long hallway ahead. It was amazing how little light actually gets through a fine window grille, Aya thought as she sniffed and sensed a strong smell of paint.

Unfamiliar with the floor layout, Aya let herself wander along the empty corridors while keeping an eye out for any directional signs.

She passed through what seemed to be the main lobby. It was covered with wall-to-wall murals, thus by a union of mind and matter singing tribute to mankind's scientific and physical achievements. A stretch of scaffolding and throw cloth partially obscured the artwork.

"Hey, hey, hey!" An angry yelp from behind her made Aya stop in her tracks and turn around.

A burly man of an undeterminable age, whose attire vaguely resembled the Yankees uniform, came out of the shadows. "Smattuhr wid yah? Did yah nahtt see dat's mah wax job yah wawkin' ahn!"

His accent was so thick it took Aya a minute to process the message. His wax job? Mr. Bumblebee must be one hard-working bee of a floor waxer.

"Whad bidness yah gaht loikin 'ere anyway?"

Good lord, buddy! Aya could barely refrain from gasping. *No wonder they got you buffing floors.* In a matter of seconds Aya assessed Mr. Bumblebee's wise career choices and all the pros and cons of attempting a two-way information exchange in a situation involving a certain dose of cultural differences. She decided the best way to close the gap was by thoroughly monopolizing every possible bit of such a conversation. To put it simply, the more she talked, the less she'd hear out of Mr. Bumblebee over there.

"Neuetech security," Aya flashed her badge.

Using big words and strange acronyms worked on most people who were too afraid to be perceived as stupid by seeking explanations for what seems to be obvious to the speaker.

"Do you always leave the back door unlocked?" Aya asked crisply.

"Only when ah leave mah pagah be'ind," Aya saw Mr. Bumblebee shift uncomfortably, his initial aggression channeling into anxiety. "Look, ah wassabeeout tah goohn grab er bitah late lunch. 'Mah in s'mkindah trouble 'ere?"

"Not that I'm aware of," Aya's voice fell back into its weary metronome. "But there's someone who is, and your cooperation, as well as the use of your keys, would serve as an invaluable boost to the mechanics of the individual's apprehension."

The moment the custodian's eyes had filled with bewilderment Aya knew how to proceed.

"If you could just direct me toward the library, I could let myself out when I'm finished," she said.

Mr. Bumblebee hesitated, then gave in. "Awl da way down, ehp da stahrs," he instructed, pointing ahead. "Six' flawr."

All the way down the corridor and up the stairs to the sixth floor, Aya mentally translated the direction and bid him farewell. "Enjoy your lunch, sir," she said and headed out in search of the stairwell.

Mr. Bumblebee's directions proved accurate. She found the library as predicted and pushed the brass door handle to let herself inside. The smell of dust was her only companion as Aya walked through the long rows of shelves in search for the school yearbooks. She located them next to the ready reference section and skimmed through the numbers etched in gold on the spines.

1985, 1986, 1987. She pulled out all three and started on the latest one first. The year of Oishi's graduation unfolded before her eyes with its extremes of studious faces and mad parties.

There were only two photographs of Oishi in the whole book; a lab scene and a portrait, neither of which appeared particularly festive. For a moment Aya simply stared at Oishi's babyish face, innocent in its look of concentration. She then read the caption under the first photograph, 'Ryuiji Oishi and Leonard Loria conducting a chemical experiment.'

Leonard Loria, Aya found the name vaguely familiar. Could he have been related to the Lorias of the hotel chain fame? Aya turned the pages toward the portrait section of the book to see if Loria's bio was attached and let out a triumphant "So he is."

She scooped the books under her arm and reached for the phone on the librarian's desk. It seemed she had a meeting to arrange.

CHAPTER XLII

He looked younger than she expected. Would that be a direct result of a lifetime full of leisure? Or mummification through extreme dieting practices? What was he, thirty-five, thirty-seven? And not a worry wrinkle across his forehead. Not a laugh line in the corners of his mouth.

He sat yoga-style in the middle of the bed, his hands resting on his knees, meditating on the mute static of the endless TV screens before him. A buddha. A god in his own compact universe – four walls, fancy purple sheets, fashionable darkness. A child, locked in a game room, desperate for a kindred soul. Of course, she would play along.

"Miss Savoy, how nice to see you." The man cut his trance short and spread his wispy arms, as if awaiting an embrace.

"Mr. Loria," Aya chose a nod of acknowledgment instead.

"Call me Leonard. Natalie, isn't it?" A string of dark hair fell across his brow, as he leaned forward to pat the side of the bed. "I could ask my assistant to fetch a chair, but I'd rather not. Would you mind?"

Aya managed a smile, a classic dumb blonde tactic, her hand testing the mattress. "Of course not."

"Of course not, Leonard," Loria took it upon himself to correct her, brushing his unruly hair away from his forehead, and giving her a glimpse of his overly thin eyebrows.

"Your name rings a bell," he then continued, unaware of Aya's appraisal of his tweezer technique. "But your face," he shook his head, "not all that familiar."

"I'm afraid the honor of attending the lavish parties of the glorious class of '87 was not bestowed upon me," she said, making herself as comfortable as her role allowed. "Besides, I was far too involved with running the school paper to have time for parties. You must've heard of me by my work."

"Ah, the young talent..." Loria fell back against an assortment of pillows at the head of the bed, his tone slipping into borderline mockery. "Such vigor, such dedication. Your basic overachiever."

"I have done well for myself if that's the implication," Aya stiffened her spine as per her role, a grossly over-acted defense reaction, which Loria acknowledged with a typical sociopathic response.

"Is that why you're here, keeping company with a benzodiazephine buff, rather than discussing latest political maneuvers with a presidential spokesman or flirting with some Australian film star?"

A sense of false superiority came twice as easily to pronounced megalomaniacs, Aya was finding out. Her trap was set. All she had to do now was watch her host take the bait, accept her as a feeble and therefore non-threatening entity, and all the dirty secrets would come spilling out.

"Is that the question that plagues you while you lie sleepless at night," Loria began. "Do I possess what it takes? Where did it all go awry? Did I not do enough backstabbing, brown-nosing? Your wardrobe is not exactly what you'd call tasteful, but the figure is plenty pretty, so what happened? Naïveté dragging you back?"

Sweet mare, mother of ten generations of ponies, the gag factor of his response turned out far worse than Aya anticipated. And here she thought she had seen every kind of creep possible. She fought back a curious combination of repulsion and laughter and waited for her gift of speech to return.

"I am here as a representative for the Brooklyn Tech yearbook committee." She resumed her role of someone who hadn't enough wit to comprehend beyond the first sentence in Loria's soliloquy. "As I informed your assistant."

"Sure." Traces of ridicule still trickled off the creep's lips. "And what is it again you wanted from me in particular?"

"I was hired to track down every last alumnus of the class of '87 and compile an account of life successes achieved by each."

"The twentieth year reunion. Right, right." Loria nodded. "They're starting early, I see. Must be Mandy Sewel's great idea. What is she now? A doctor? A lawyer? A money grabber of some other sort? Still, nineteen years, who would imagine it's been that long...."

For a moment he fell silent, overpowered by memories, then resumed with added cheer. "So you're here for my story. There's not much to tell, I fear. As you can see for yourself, I've been relieved of the necessity to fight for a success of my own. I inherited one the moment my dear stepmother put a slug into my cheating dog of a father. Are you taping this?"

"Eidetic memory." Aya pointed in the general direction of her head.

"I should've known," Loria shrugged before getting back on track. "Anyway, my father willed it all to me. No matter how much of a fuck-up he thought I was. Blood ties tug the strongest when one senses his near demise. I believe he did, my father. I believe most people get that sneaky feeling before they are about to meet their final end. Like a sick animal crawling off to die, father knew way before mother-dear finally lost it and reached for that gun. A prolonged coma and then no more," Loria's smile was one of pity, yet something in the darkness of his eyes kept Aya from buying into his seeming sincerity.

"Anything else you'd like to know?"

Before she had time to decide on the validity of Loria's human dogs hypothesis, his mood, whether real or pretend, suddenly flipped back to taunting. "Would you like to hear about my hobbies? They include reading new age books, bloodhounds, (which I do not own,) and electronics. I am single, fun-loving, suffering from multiple social disorders, including a slight case of agoraphobia, and ingesting antidepressants and other novel compounds by mouth twice a day. Will the committee find this information satisfactory?"

"Very much so. And I do hope your fellow alumni prove to be as frank as yourself."

"Prove to be?" Loria's wit fell limp at the sight of Aya's straight face, agitation at his failure to provoke a colorful reaction getting the best of him. "Meaning I am the first one on your list? I'm flattered."

"Second, actually. Ryuiji Oishi could not be reached."

Loria flushed, as if offended at not being the first one on her list. "Why don't you try some mental wards?" he scoffed. "Or better yet, don't waste your precious time looking. I could tell you all about him myself. More than you'd ever care to know."

Please do, Aya's patience was running thin, *do us both a favor.* She pursed her lips for what she hoped was one last time and, weary of the charade, tried not to let the desire to castrate the pathetic bastard overwhelm her entirely.

"Oishi, a perpetual geek-boy," Loria spat in contempt. "Obsessed with conspiracy theories concerning his parents' demise. The folks were driving home drunk, got themselves into a wreck. Bam! Dead. As simple as that. Always is. The crazy idiot went ballistic, convinced they were abducted, experimented on and assassinated, not necessarily in that order. Not sure who he blamed. Don't care. Could be the extraterrestrials, I wouldn't be surprised. How's that for a character study? Had enough?"

Enough? *Was* it enough for Aya's purposes? It was about all the freak could offer to outlive his usefulness. It was enough to give Aya a rough idea. And *that* would have to do.

"Now." Loria gave a wry grin as his mind-set underwent another makeover, shifting back to megalomaniacal grandeur. "My psychiatrist recommends I try dining in female company, so what do you say to dinner?"

Oh, the things she was dying to say....

CHAPTER XLIII

Waiting on the sidewalk, Wade finally spotted Aya's slender form appear from the depths of the Loria Inn lobby and, as her hand reached for the revolving door, he gave the gilded contraption a concurrent spin from the other side.

For a moment positively stupefied, Aya regarded Wade through the glass, then stepped aside, allowing him to enter. "Gavin," she managed to say despite her astonishment. "What d'you know?"

"Small world." He shielded himself with clichés while his eyes adjusted to the less-than-sunny interior.

Aya smiled and gave him a sideways hug, the scent of her perfume ever so potent at dissolving his earlier resolve toward emotional detachment.

"The Bureau still on my ass?" She pulled away to probe at the nature of what had brought them together.

"No, no." Wade shook his head. "I believe it's safe to say they're officially over the calamity that is you."

She smiled again and touched at his wrist gently, as if to

175

prompt further elaboration.

"I'm here on an entirely different matter." He provided what she sought to hear and, however superficial, his response seemed to put her suspicions at rest for the time being.

"Working cases, going places...."

"You?" Wade shifted the focus of the conversation away from himself.

"Just through declining a dinner proposal from a megalomaniacal dickweed of an acquaintance and back to believing in lucky chances. You're staying here, in this hotel?"

Wade nodded affirmatively.

"Tax dollars at work, huh?" Aya threw in a bit of mockery. "A room must be what, five hundred a night? More?"

"Complimentary as per service agreement." Wade went with a sensible reply.

"Way to go!" she exclaimed. "Does that include the hookers?" Seemingly unaware of her ability to make him blush, Aya suddenly discarded her wisecracking attitude in favor of patting her stomach. "Second thoughts about that dinner proposal," she explained. "I'd better get some chow to shut that puppy up. Hey, it's been nice seeing you again."

Wade grunted unintelligibly before she turned to walk away.

"Keep your nose clean, huh?" Aya's hand once again tried the door handle, when Wade called to her.

"The work agreement I mentioned earlier," he said. "It includes complimentary meals as well."

***

Once settled at the table Aya grabbed a menu and perused it

with as much concentration as if the choice of entree contained all the secrets to the afterlife.

Wade didn't feel particularly hungry. Nor was he interested in discovering the secrets to the afterlife. He decided on his order without either ado or care and watched Aya carry on her scrutiny (that little wrinkle between her eyebrows, long lashes casting a jagged shadow) his head full of questions, only a minute increment of which he could ever dare to voice. "So I presume the job offer in Arizona fell through?"

"No, I got it actually." Aya put the menu back in the tray, the corners of her lips displaying a polite elevation. "Security with a big company. You can imagine how that is. Way too much travel, way too many conferences for my taste. Been cooped up all day long with one lousy sub at lunchtime. You know, some people just don't bother to make allowances for a high metabolic rate."

"You, sitting through a conference?" Wade teased, fully aware she was lying. "Come on, where's the real Aya? What have you done to her?"

"Well, maybe I didn't sit through the entire thing. I say half a day is better than none at all. Besides, I doubt anybody noticed my stealthy getaway." She broke off to greet the arrival of their beverages, then picked up where she left off. "But enough about me. What kind of a case are you working on?"

Wade faltered, wondering if the question had emerged out of the realm of suspicion. But Aya's exultation at the sight of the waiter's cart seemed much too real to involve calculating intent.

"Extortion." Wade went with the truth as the means of getting Aya's reaction, but her face produced no visible effect, and Wade found himself no closer to overcoming her lies.

"Hmm." Her mouth was utterly preoccupied with grilled

chicken. "I hope..." she swallowed. "...I do hope it's something more involved than a fat cat getting busted with his pants down."

Perhaps, she knew less than he thought.

"Any leads?" she asked.

Then again, Aya was a first-rate actress, and Wade decided against sharing further details. "Oh yes, plenty of leads. Although too early to tell which one will play out in the end."

She waved her fork, about to resume cutting and stabbing. "I'm sure you'll do fine. You've always been the talented one." She beamed, ready for the next bite. "The pride and joy of DC."

Wade scoffed, and an awkward silence commenced. Done with his meal, though not finished, he put his cutlery aside, only to realize he hadn't another thing to say. All the questions he had wanted to ask suddenly made no sense.

He took a sip of water, an increasing certainty that it was he who had to revive the conversation bearing down on him. He was the one who had to set the course and control it. Instead he drew a blank and panicked. By the time the words escaped his lips it was too late to do anything but regret them. "Are you happy?" he heard his own voice say, though it took his mind a moment to catch up.

Surely, he hadn't really said the words out loud but had just whispered them in his mind. But Aya's face, which suddenly assumed that familiar unreadable expression as she shut the world out, brought Wade to reality.

Oh god, he cringed inside. Those words *had* come out of his mouth. Why, why had he asked such a question? Was it even in his thoughts before it had slipped off his tongue? Wade had no choice but to follow the conversation in the direction he had inadvertently steered it and wait for Aya's reply.

"Of course, I'm happy, Gavin," she pronounced vacantly. "I am a balanced, integrated soul. Why wouldn't I be happy?" Quite in contrast to her tone she added a playful wink. "You've known me a while, longer than just about anyone else. You shouldn't have to ask."

Yes, she looked happy enough. Happy in her indifference, in her flirtation with the cuisine. She was happy to be inventing nonexistent conferences and mingling with suspected extortionists.

She was a natural liar. Wade was almost compelled to believe her words rather than his own eyes. Yet he recognized the signs. All those times he had seen her work her magic on the job, that icy self-control, the occasional gentle encouragement. He admired her skill. But being on the receiving end of her lies was something quite different from watching her as her partner.

"Five years," he acknowledged. "And sometimes I still wonder if fifty is enough to know who you are."

Aya stopped plowing through what was left of her mashed potatoes, her fork frozen in midair. Visibly taken aback, she stared at Wade, but only for a fragment of a second. Then she burst out laughing. "Was that your diplomatic way of calling me a secretive bitch?" she said through the laughter. "Good lord, Gavin. I leave you on your own for a month and here you are calling me names already."

In spite of himself Wade felt his face redden once again, and he was grateful when Aya's cell phone diverted her attention elsewhere. She reached to check the caller ID and, despite the disapproving glances from the highbrows at the adjoining tables, let the phone continue to ring. "Duty calls," she said as she pushed her chair back. "I'm sorry, Gavin, I have to take this."

179

He gave an empathetic nod and watched her walk away toward the waiting area.

CHAPTER XLIV

With Wade safely out of hearing range, Aya picked up her phone. "Morell here."

"How nice to hear your voice again." She heard Oishi's courteous greeting on the other end of the line. "I'm not interrupting anything, am I?" He prodded at the time it took her to answer the phone.

Aya looked back at Wade, waiting for her at the table, and walked farther away from the seating area of the restaurant. "Hardly," she said.

"Good. Then we could meet."

"Tonight?" she asked, somewhat surprised at the promptness of his decision.

"Ready when you are." Oishi's answer sounded a lot like an invitation for a game of hide and seek. "Does half an hour from now sound good?"

"Where?" Aya saved all her other questions for later.

"Central Park looks beautiful at this time of day. Why don't you wait for me at the Angel of the Waters?"

"I'll be there," she promised before disconnecting, and turned back toward the dining hall.

***

Wade got up from the table as she approached. He looked tired and worried, but Aya was in too much of a rush to pry.

"Bad news?" he asked.

"Looks like I might be in trouble for skipping that conference today." She quickly came up with a lie. "I'm sorry to be running out on you like this, but I'm afraid now I have to go and face the music."

"Yeah, I understand." He didn't ask for details.

"Thanks for the dinner anyway." She patted him on the shoulder and smiled. "Still friends?"

"Still friends," he agreed without sharing her smile.

CHAPTER XLV

Aya sat down on the rim of the fountain and admired the early sunset over Bethesda Terrace. The Angel of the Waters towered behind her, its cascading murmur comfortingly annoying. Something felt amiss.

Running into Wade was one. What were the odds regarding their encounter? One in ten million? Astronomical? Wouldn't the equation be a lot simpler if a certain degree of plotting was involved?

Was the Bureau on her tail? She had seen no one following her, but then again the subtle art of spotting tails had never been Aya's strongest suit.

Oishi's call was another oddity. His sudden willingness to meet was in contrast to his seeming disappointment with their prior conversation. He had wanted her to learn about his parents. He had gone so far as making that knowledge a condition of their next meeting. And although Aya had honored his request, he could have no way of knowing that without asking. He hadn't asked, he had offered no more mention of his parents' existence.

183

Shouldn't the question have been the first thing to come out of his mouth when he had called her? What had changed? Did he not care anymore? Or was it that he knew of Aya's actions without having to ask? His friends had been watching her prior to their first meeting, were they still? Had they been following her every move?

"Voyeurism, is that a newly-acquired hobby of yours?" Aya tested her theory, as Oishi walked down the stone steps toward her.

"I admit the whole routine was not altogether unpleasant." He didn't attempt to deny the allegation. He only flashed an apologetic smile and sat down beside her.

"Then you already know what it is I have to say. And I, apparently, have passed the test." Aya turned sideways to face her interlocutor, but found him staring off in the distance, his countenance suddenly grim.

"Jen Collins was her name," Oishi began, as if obeying some ghostly prompt. "She was fifteen. What you'd call a bad girl. She took a liking to me, or maybe it was all a ploy to make fun of the shy foreign boy. I'll never know.

"There was a party going on that night, one of Jen's snobby girlfriends' moms was away on a cruise with her masseuse; daddy was putting in long hours with his new secretary. Booze, loud music, swimming pool, what else could you wish for? I was miserably pissed, even before the punch line (if there was to be one) and Jen had to take me home, so I wouldn't ruin the upholstery.

"I climbed back in my bedroom window and ran to the bathroom to throw up. As my stomach cramps subsided, I heard my parents' voices in the living room. Still queasy, I crept down the hall and peeked around the corner to see what was going on. I figured my little escape had been discovered, but they weren't tears of anger running down my mother's cheeks. They were that of sorrow, fear.

"'Watashe kowaiwa,' she said. 'I'm scared.' And my father held her, mumbling, 'They wouldn't dare, they wouldn't dare.'

"Those were the last words I heard my parents speak. The last time I saw them alive." Oishi paused, for a moment lost in the raspberry afterglow of the sunset, his weak grin only accentuating the despair of his loss.

"Their car was found next morning by the side of the road. The police report said it was an accidental rollover – the steering wheel was turned too sharply to avoid a collision with someone or something. But there was no further evidence; no witnesses ever came forth, no explanation as to why they had left the house in the middle of the night. Except for..." Oishi held the pause before spitting out the answer. "They were already dead before they reached that car, weren't they? And the only reason I'm still here, alive, is that I was passed out in the bathroom, too insignificant, too pathetic to bother with."

Aya gave him time to collect his thoughts before she expressed her bewilderment. "But why do you think Neuetech was involved? Why not hundreds of other shady operations?"

"Prior to his death, my father worked for a pharmaceutical outfit by the name of Cornell-Warren, Ltd. I was thirteen when it all started. The phone calls, strange people coming over to our house late at night, my father jumping in fear at the sound of closing doors. He called me into his office about a month before he died, he said he wanted to tell me something important and he needed me to listen. He said he was having some trouble at work, he was looking into a matter he was not supposed to know about, and certain people at his company were rather insistent that he not investigate. But my father couldn't stop, he believed the matter concerned his professional honor. He asked me, as one man of another, to take care of my mother, if something were to happen to him. I was young, but not too young to understand.

"Cornell-Warren went belly up in the mid-eighties. Its core staff, however, wasn't out in the cold for long before being promptly recruited by a Dr. Gail Hager. And that's when I knew my calling in life."

"Chemical engineering," Aya said.

"That was the plan," Oishi nodded.

"Getting a job at Neuetech, then sinking it from within."

"I was amazed at how easy it actually was. No one suspected. My father's occupation, my being where I was made legitimate sense. And after years of lies and pretense, I had that disk in my hand, the moment my life had been leading up to.

"But instead of a triumphant bliss, all I felt coming over me was the realization of the purposelessness of my battle. I had won, the CEO's would take the stand, the guilty would be punished. But only to clear the niche for a hundred others.

"My parents were dead, nothing was going to change that. For the first time the thought hit me hard. Something had changed somewhere along the way. Vengeance no longer possessed its appeal, its purity. *I* changed.

"Countless instances of justifying questionable means had tainted my sacred intentions. Lies had become a habit, a second nature to follow. My defeat was of my own making and ever so irreversible."

"So you chose the worldly goods over your father's

memory." Aya summed it up.

Oishi remained silent.

"What about Dannii?"

"The lucky one. She's in it for the money and she knows it." Oishi scoffed with the contempt one might display toward leeches. "Dannii approached me about a year ago, I doubt that's her real name, by the way. She said she had done a few freelance jobs here and there, information exchange type of thing. She said she knew Neuetech was dirty, she wanted to see them pay. Dannii was the one who came up with the plan and gave me the tools to go through with it. Of course, I knew she wasn't just helping me out of the goodness of her heart, but as long as she could help me get the evidence I needed, I accepted her as a necessary evil."

"And Sitar Player?" Aya asked.

"You don't actually believe it was the horse I was putting up for sale?"

"Company secrets?"

"I thought I'd offer Maltais the luxury of the first bid. But he chose to send you instead."

"He didn't," Aya begged to differ.

"How's that?"

"I suppose I did my job better than he expected a woman to manage. I suppose, I interrupted something without knowing it."

She should've seen it earlier. The hotel, the special treatment, the whole reasoning behind her hire. She had been chosen because of the baggage to her reputation. She had been hired to fail. To serve as a scapegoat, while Maltais got off clean and kept the disk for himself.

"Maltais is like a mammoth, holding on to old dogmas,

187

without yet realizing that his kind is headed for extinction. He appears to believe that women are an inferior herd. Is that why you keep Dannii around?"

Oishi remained silent once again.

"What's on the disk?" Aya demanded.

"Why ask when you already have the answer?" Oishi's tone brought to mind an almost Buddhist-style treatment of the obvious.

"Do I?"

"You've seen what it does. You know what it's for. Something the humble field of prosthetics could only dream of."

"What are you talking about?" Aya was getting tired of second-guessing.

"I am talking about what you saw at the New River Road facility."

"L-2?"

"First you try, then you fail before finally succeeding. Research, application, marketing. Three branch levels of a healthy technological body." Oishi unveiled the meaning behind the abbreviation. "Now why don't you tell me about what you saw. It'll make you feel better, I promise."

CHAPTER XLVI

What exactly had she seen down in the belly of the New River Road facility? Aya wasn't sure she knew the answer herself. It all seemed like a distant dream now, the desert, the gas station, Ronnie's bewildered face.

She had seen something that could not possibly be real. Something so perverted in its nature, it could not possibly exist. And Aya refused to believe it had ever been there.

"What did you see?" As if through deep water, she heard Oishi's voice, filled with reassurance, and re-connected with the present.

"I don't know." She shook her head, suddenly feeling as if she were about to fall apart. Aya was still looking away, when Oishi's hand cupped hers. Was that another thing to make her feel better? Why would he even care about the way she felt?

Aya pulled away.

"Andrea Wallace worked as a mailroom clerk in the Neuetech Arizona offices." Oishi spoke after a moment of silence. "Poor child. She was nineteen when a neuroblastoma

189

metastasized to her liver. The news extinguished her will to struggle on. She was found in her bathtub, wrists slit, barely breathing. I don't know how Neuetech ended up with the body, but I'm sure that expenditure was kept off the books.

"They used axolotl DNA to rebuild, or rather re-grow her internal organs that had been eaten away by cancer. As well as her hands, which had to be removed post-mortem, on account of extensive tissue damage.

"A fascinating creature, axolotl. It is a spotted salamander that possesses the gift of regeneration. The trick about adopting the process to fit human specification, though, is suppressing those pesky cellular mutations. But Andrea was the first, and deviations were hardly the main point of concern then. Neuetech was much too preoccupied with slicing through Andrea's skull cap to try and restore the basic functions of her nervous system."

"She is kept locked up in a box, like an animal," Aya interrupted, taken aback by Oishi's blend of compassion and cynicism.

"Insisting she's other than an animal would be a bit of a stretch in the circumstances," he replied. "Everything Andrea was, her hopes, her dreams, vanished forever when brain death occurred. Now she is just a mangled shell with all the intelligence of an aquatic lizard." His words tumbled out hard, like profanity in church.

"So that's what's on the disk? A recipe for creating half-breeds?"

"Potential immortality," Oishi corrected, rubbing his hands together. "By the way, my curiosity is getting the best of me. How did you manage to sneak inside the facility undetected? No, wait, let me guess. The lax delivery procedure, am I right? That's how I would've done it," he continued. "The only thing about that is there is no way you could've been unseen."

"I don't know what you're talking about." Aya, her defenses back in place, had no inclination to make confessions.

Oishi gave a short snort, as he derived the true order of events all the same. "The delivery boy, perhaps the store clerk, the acquisitions guy, your nerdy tag-along pal..." He shook his head. "Pretty brutal. But I suppose, you had no other choice. If you had let them live, your own life wouldn't be worth a penny. Your friend could've talked about where you'd been, and you couldn't risk being found out."

"I don't know what you're talking about," Aya repeated.

"What if I said you could have the disk?" Oishi's face lit up with a smirk. "What would you do if I gave it to you? Would you return it to Neuetech, justice restored? Or would you screw everyone over (not that any of our mutual acquaintances don't deserve it) and cash in?"

He leaned forward to see Aya's expression. "I bet you'd choose the money. I bet you would." His hand reached toward her; his fingers caught a loose strand of her hair, ran through it down to her cheek. "You do find it familiar, don't you? Choosing questionable methods to punish the wrongdoers. Battling fire with fire, unaware that your own self is being consumed by it as well. But there comes a time..." Without finishing his thought Oishi leaned further forward and kissed Aya's lips.

She closed her eyes, though the kiss was brief and the feeling fleeting, and listened to her conscience whisper with his warm breath at her neck.

"You may choose to ignore what you are, you may choose to try and stop me. But wouldn't you rather come to terms with your own nature? A decision that is entirely yours to make."

CHAPTER XLVII

"Dammit, Morell, why don't you answer your phone?" The tone of Maltais' voice belied the agitation of his words. "I thought you were dead as well."

"Dead?" Aya echoed, half-wishing she hadn't powered her phone back on.

"Going by that eloquently expressed, uninformed awe, I gather you've been spared the inconvenience of witnessing the event, but our man was, in fact, shot dead in your hotel room." The bigoted bastard was clearly enjoying playing up her ignorance. "Two bullets to the chest. Nice and tidy. I doubt he even knew what hit him."

The shadow man Maltais had so generously hired for Aya's so-called protection had been murdered in her room. There it was, the reason Oishi warned her against going back to the hotel. The reason he felt sure she was no longer being followed.

Kudos, Oishi. The caterpillar completes its cycle, as a tragic, misunderstood hero gives way for a cold-blooded killer to emerge. Such is life.

Where did he learn his clean game anyway? Taking out a trained operative without breaking a sweat, without getting caught? Something that only comes with practice. Or would the loss of one's parents suffice?

"Whoever it was, they must've gone through your luggage as well. Hope you didn't keep a diary."

"Whoever it was?" Aya preferred to ignore Maltais' final remark and took a stab at his professional competency instead. "Meaning, you have no clue as to who actually killed him?"

"Feel free to have a wild guess."

Arrogant bastard. Perhaps, it hadn't been Oishi after all who had done the killing. For one thing, there would simply not have been enough time for him to comb through Aya's entire stash of extra underwear and still make the Da Silvano appointment. Even if he had waited outside the hotel doors for her to leave, there was still the matter of travel time to be considered. Otherwise he would've been very late.

Oishi hadn't been very late. Which left Aya with one other alternative. He'd had help. Dannii, perhaps. Or if not her, then someone else of her kind.

"Where are you now?" Aya blurted out into the receiver.

"Meeting Oishi," came a cool reply from the opposite side of the line. "He contacted us a couple of hours ago ready to make a deal."

"Where?"

"I don't see how it would matter for you to know now," he said in that patronizing tone again. "It's this piece of shit warehouse in Bayonne. But Oishi is due to arrive any minute, so don't try to make it here. We've got it all under control, don't worry. Just a simple exchange. He'll get his money, I'll get the disk. It's over. Relax, go have a drink. You've done a great job. We're flying back to Phoenix tomorrow morning. Don't worry, it's all been taken care of."

Aya was getting quite tired of all the 'don't worry's.' "Where in Bayonne?"

She heard Maltais sigh. "East 36th Street. Not that it makes any difference. Like I said, there's no need for you to be here.

"By the way, where have you been all this time?" he added after a slight pause, but didn't wait for an answer. "Never mind that, I'll call you later tonight," he dismissed her and hung up.

So it was all over. Aya exhaled, feeling like she had missed the best part. But then she had indeed. She was missing it right then, as Maltais was going to apprehend Oishi without her.

Was he actually going to apprehend Oishi? How odd, he'd mentioned nothing of his plans for Oishi's apprehension over the phone. Was he going to let Oishi go? Complete the exchange, give him the money and just let him go? Let him get away with it?

Maltais had said 'we've got it under control.' Who was 'we?' More agents like the dead man in Aya's room? Then surely they were planning on catching Oishi red-handed. Of course, they were.

Everything was under control.

Aya took another long breath as the dusk was beginning to set in. The phone still in her hand, she checked for Maltais' messages. There were three messages in all. Two from Maltais' cell phone; one from somewhere in Phoenix. Aya punched in her pass code and pressed 'one' to play.

"Hi, this is Melanie Holt speaking."

One sentence was enough for Aya to pin down that raspy

voice, although the name did not ring a bell. Melanie, so that's what she was called, the melancholy clerk from the 7th Street Marriott.

"We've run into some trouble retrieving the records you asked for. The list of our guests from Neuetech seems to be inaccessible. We'll keep working on it if you still need that information, but so far all I have is something the manager happened to remember on his own. About a year ago we had Miss Dannii Hartwell, a real pretty..."

Aya didn't listen to the rest of the message. Dannii? *The* Dannii? On Neuetech's payroll? What were the odds of a different woman with the same name working for Neuetech? The name was not exactly that common.

But if it were the Dannii, the elusive Dannii, why hadn't she changed her name? Was it because that was the way she was known to Oishi when they met? Had she met Oishi at the 7th Street Marriott? Was she still on Neuetech's payroll? Is that why the records of her stay proved impossible to retrieve?

Would she be by Oishi's side when the exchange took place tonight? Or would she be helping Maltais? Did Oishi know? Did he have his own agenda drawn out as well? Was Aya the only one who wasn't bringing a bag of tricks?

She hooked her cell phone back on her belt and ran toward 5th Avenue. "There's an old warehouse on the East 36th in Bayonne," she shouted into the window of the first cab she could spot. "I need to be there five minutes ago."

CHAPTER XLVIII

As Wade stood watching from across the canal, it all suddenly made sense. Aya's secrecy, the hiding, her lies, all suddenly made sense when she accepted that kiss. She was not investigating the case, she was a part of it, in on it.

Oh sure, she might have been just trying to gain the suspect's trust. Sure, their conversation might have been quite lengthy due to the amount of valuable tips she had been receiving. Sure, the moon was made of marshmallows, and pigs took up extensive flying lessons.

Nightfall was imminent by the time the man finally left, the last licks of the sunset rippling through the water. Aya lingered by the side of the fountain, preoccupied with her phone. Wade shifted his weight around, his legs getting stiff from the lack of movement, his shoulder irritated by the prolonged contact with the deep grooves of the oak tree bark. He blinked. Had he dozed off for a moment? He must have, for the next thing he knew Aya was off and running for a cab.

Wade jumped out from behind the tree where he had been

197

hiding and rushed after her. Why was she running? he wondered as he crossed the short, metal bridge over the canal. And where? Was she trying to catch up with her friend? Was it something to do with her phone? Had she received a summons?

Wherever she was headed, Wade was going to have to figure out the reasons on his way there.

***

The taxi dropped her off at an old shipyard. Wade's cabby killed the headlights and pulled over a good hundred yards up the road while Aya made her way toward the dark shadow of a large warehouse ahead. The weak moonlight painted the outline of the building the palest of grays, downgrading the surrounding objects and structures to mere shapes, forms without depth. The ghostly grounds at a haunted hour, Aya walked upon them like an unearthly spirit before her silhouette vanished inside the warehouse door.

Wade let his cabby go and started to follow her, but he stopped in his tracks before he had a chance to reach his destination. A sedan parked behind an old railroad car caught his attention. There was movement inside. Wade approached the car.

Aya's pals there to meet her, Wade guessed. Well, they might not make it to their rendezvous point quite so soon. Not before Wade had a little chat with them. As Wade crept closer, he was able to make out a single occupant inside the sedan. A man. Was it the same one he had seen in Aya's company earlier? Was the scenario that predictable?

Wade reached down in his holster, waiting for the sedan's

door to open. "Hold it right there," he called out, before the driver had time to fully exit the car.

The man froze in place, his head at half-turn. Unlike Aya's friend in the park, the man was Caucasian. He was tall, at least six foot three, solidly built under his expensive suit. And, Wade noted, he was armed.

"Drop it. Hands where I can see them," Wade barked.

The man complied by letting his gun fall to the ground. Wade kicked it away and circled around to face his opponent.

"Who are you?" the man asked dryly.

"FBI, pal." Wade flashed his badge. "I'd like to hear your take on what's going on here. Sort of like a celebrity interview, and you're the star. Action; go."

The man sized him up with a smirk. "Neuetech Securities, pal. Investigating an internal matter."

"Never heard of them."

"My ID badge is in the pocket of my jacket. Help yourself."

"Toward the car, hands on the hood, legs apart." Wade followed the standard procedure.

The man once again complied. Such was the power of the Glock in Wade's hand.

It was only when Wade approached to administer a pat down that the man's elbow swung back and upward, faster than a cat's paw. The blow glanced off Wade's jaw, leaving him disoriented as the taste of blood from his broken lip filled his mouth. He saw the man dash to recover the discarded gun, but before possible became real, Wade beat him to the punch. He moved to hit the man on the back of the head with the butt of his Glock, and his opponent slumped, unconscious, against the sedan's front wheel.

Wade took a minute to catch his breath and then went through the contents of the man's pockets. He found a pair of handcuffs, a set of keys, a wallet full of credit cards and ID's that proved the man was indeed Conrad Maltais, the Chief of Security of Neuetech Industries, Southwest Division. An Arizona driver's license was visible through the clear plastic window on the side of the wallet.

Arizona, private securities, could that be Aya's boss Wade had just knocked out cold? Such a small world. Was he there to assist Aya in apprehending the bad guy? Was he there to apprehend Aya? Whose side was he on anyway? Clearly, there were too many sides to keep track of.

Either way, assaulting an officer of the law was a crime the last time Wade had checked and his new friend, if he weren't slumbering, would have been beyond doubt excited to learn of his impending trip to the jailhouse. Wade handcuffed his suspect to the steering wheel, got out his cell phone and dialed information for the NYPD contact number. He could use some local police presence on this one.

Everything would sort itself out in the end, Wade was sure.

CHAPTER XLIX

It was cumbersomely dark by the time Aya reached the warehouse, the cranes and forklifts ominous shadows in the cab's headlights. Naked masts reaching for the pale stars. The shipyards waiting in silence for the sun to return.

"You want me to wait for you?" The cabby rolled down the window and leaned across the passenger seat.

"That won't be necessary, thanks."

As the sound of the taxi's engine died away, Aya set off across the railroad tracks toward the dark mass of the warehouse. In the dim light of the crescent moon, she spotted a car parked by the entrance gate to the hangar, an Audi, its hood still warm from recent use. Did it belong to Oishi? Was Maltais already inside? Was she too late? Too late for what? Oishi's arrest? Oishi's leave taking? Maltais' triumph in one way or another?

Aya felt a chain threaded through the hasp on the hangar's door, but it was not padlocked in place, and the door rattled ajar as she pushed. Kimber close at hand, she stepped inside.

Was the property even in active use anymore? The interior of the hangar, generously endowed with extra footage (or did it only *seem* endless in the near dark), was empty except for a mid-size sailboat resting on top of cast steel bilge blocks toward the front section of the premises. Lit from the port side by a faint source out of the tool storage room beyond, the scrubbed-down keel gave off a dull eerie shine. Aya looked up, only to see the bowsprit hanging over her head, the boat's rigging disappearing into the pitch-black of the ceiling.

She suddenly felt as if she were underwater, walking along the bottom of the sea, the sounds of the world above muffled by a million gallons of water. A feeling desperate in its finality, yet comforting for one and the same reason. Like an act of surrender that fills the heart with a sense of failure, yet provides simultaneous relief for not having to face more tribulations, that place at the bottom of the sea has all the peace to offer. And like a good priest, it keeps your secrets safe.

"I remember you." There was a movement by the storage room and a young woman (a mermaid?) appeared out of the shadows. Positively striking in a pinstripe suit (whoever heard of a mermaid armed with a .38?), the woman threw back her mane of black hair, the long curve of her lip oddly familiar.

Dannii, Aya presumed with a prick of jealousy. That's who the Audi outside belonged to, Dannii.

"Where's Maltais?" The barrel of the woman's gun was pointed at Aya.

Where's Maltais? What sort of a question was that? Wasn't Maltais supposed to be there already? Or so he had said on the phone. Or was he lying in wait for Oishi to show up first?

"Running late," Aya said and lowered her weapon.

Dannii followed Aya's lead and put her gun down to

retrieve a jewel case out of her pocket. "Not too late to miss out on this, I hope." She gave the case a demonstrative shake. "Had to pry it out of Ryuiji's clammy hands."

The way she moved, the seductive smile that followed, that languorously disconcerting manner was all unmistakably familiar. But Aya had never met Dannii face to face before. Or had she?

"By the way, you can tell Maltais I'm sick and tired of his chauvinist ways." Dannii slipped the disk back into her pocket. "And of his uncoordinated staff. This is the last job I do for him."

Aya struggled to recall where she had seen the woman before.

"As soon as I get the money, we're through."

Aya suddenly remembered the brunette in the stands at Turf Paradise, holding a brochure up to her face. She must've known what Aya looked like, she must've recognized her. Had she been acting on Maltais' orders when she had followed Aya to the stables and knocked her out cold?

"So how about it?" Dannii's impatient gesture brought Aya back to the present. "The money?"

"Oishi?" Aya deflected.

Dannii's hand pointed into the dark, toward the stern of the sailboat.

"He's a bit roughed up at the moment, sorry about that."

Oishi was in the building? Why wouldn't he show himself then? And what about Maltais?

For a moment lost in confusion, Aya dove into the depth of the shadows in search of answers. She found Oishi, lying motionless on the floor by the bilge blocks, arms tied behind his back. Aya knelt down to check his neck for pulse. Her fingers came away bloody.

"He's been shot." Aya turned around without getting up.

Dannii stood, leaning against the accommodation ladder of the sailboat, her silhouette accentuated by the dull yellow light. "Just a flesh wound. A couple of stitches and he'll be up and running, ready to decode those precious files so Maltais can have his world on a platter. And by the way, I'm sorry about your head the last time we met." She swept her hair aside once again, her voice going from an intimate whisper of apologies into a higher pitch.

"Now, I've kept my end of the bargain, so where is Maltais and where is..." Dannii paused, then screamed out the remainder of the sentence, "...my money?!"

Dannii raised her .38 and took aim, the barrel shaky in her grip. Aya rolled to the side, her Kimber firmly in her hand. Dannii's dark eyes flew open in an adrenaline rush, as the sound of the gunfire bounced off the hangar's tin walls with a deafening echo. Dannii's head shot back. She staggered and fell over onto the concrete floor, the .38 bouncing aside with a clank as it hit the ground.

Aya got up, Kimber still steady in her hand, and approached Dannii's limp body to examine the damage. Couldn't be much deader, she concluded and turned her lifeless adversary over on one side to recover the disk. Dannii's long hair slipped forward, revealing a tattoo that decorated the back of her neck. A string of dancing black cats, how third-grade, Aya thought and reached over to retrieve the disk. It was still intact, undamaged by Dannii's fall. Aya stuck it behind her belt and helped herself to Dannii's car keys.

She felt a slight soreness in her hip due to the recent

acrobatics, but her rear end had been bound to befriend the concrete sooner or later, Aya knew that much, and better sooner and of her own initiative than later, when she had run out of ways to deflect Dannii's questions. Aya dusted off her skirt and took out her knife to cut Oishi loose.

"Aren't you a sight to behold." A familiar voice out of the dark, distorted by the void of the hangar, interrupted her progress. "I suppose you shot in self-defense?"

Oishi slumped back down to the floor as Aya stood with her hands above her head and waited for the intruder to step into the light. "Gavin." Her incredulous exhale turned mid-way into a scoff. "I should've known. Another coincidence? Two in one day seems like an awful lot."

He made a face. One of those half-scornful, half-amused puppy faces he was so fond of.

His lip was bleeding.

His shirttail was out.

His hair was a mess.

He was holding a gun.

"You've been making good use of your time, I see." Without lowering his weapon, Wade approached Dannii's body and kicked it over on its back for the purpose of visual identification.

"Another perfect ten." He inspected the bullet hole in Dannii's forehead, his eyes staying on it almost a little too long to be mere detective work. "Never go for the cheap shots, do you?"

"You've been following me. Why?"

"Because you seem to enjoy some shady company." He nodded toward Oishi lying prone at her feet.

"It's a job, Gavin. And anyway, I'm taking him in." She made a motion forward, despite his grimace of disbelief.

"Stop." He cut her advance short. "The local police are on their way. They'll take care of the problem for you."

"You going to shoot, Gavin?"

"Not if you do as I say, I won't." He ignored her smirk and played it straight.

"Good, because *I* am." With a sweeping motion Aya grabbed the Kimber from under her belt and released the safety. "Drop your gun and back away against the wall. Do it now!"

Wade didn't make a move. He spoke calmly, his aim still clear. "You got too close, didn't you? We all do at one point or another. If you wrestle the monster long enough, you're bound to pick up some fleas. Walk the line once too many times, and you might forget to appreciate the balance it provides. But you don't have to. It's not the only choice you have. Do you think there's glamour in big crime?"

"Don't start with me, Gavin," she warned.

He ignored her.

"It's dirty. It's ugly. You don't flirt with crime. You don't tell yourself 'this one time only, just one hefty score.' You don't walk away from it, don't retire rich. Once the line is crossed, there's no turning back, you're no longer in control. Your deed owns you. It puts a lien against your soul and body, and you end up dead on the floor of an abandoned warehouse." Wade tilted his head toward Dannii's lifeless shape.

"Shut up," Aya hissed, unable to contain her spite.

He ignored her. "That man, you don't honestly expect me to believe you were taking him in. Oh no. You want something from him. Something he has. You want it for yourself, whatever it is. How much is it worth, Aya? Enough to sell your soul to get it?"

"Shut up, Gavin." Her voice remained a whisper of contempt. "You're no one to preach. Living in dreamland. You're just as full of it as the rest of the fumbling idiots. You're just a little academy brat with your color-blind views on honesty and success. Did you know they all laugh at you behind your back? I bet Tieri sent you off because he was sick of hearing you whine. That's all you ever do. You don't catch criminals; you nag them to death. Well, don't expect me to drop dead from your whining alone."

Something punched at Aya's right shoulder. Hard. She took an involuntary step backward, almost twisting her ankle in her high heel shoes, when the sharp pain caught up with her and her knees buckled. Aya's fingers suddenly refused to retain their hold on the gun's grip, and the Kimber slipped out of her hand and slid across the concrete floor.

The son of a bitch had shot her. She would never have imagined he'd had it in him. The fucking, cutesy, puppy-eyed bastard had pulled the trigger.

Aya had never been wounded in the line of duty, some would say, because she was always quick on the draw. She preferred to think of it as being careful not to underestimate her opponent. But there was a first time for everything. And boy, had she underestimated Wade. Her head spinning, Aya's legs finally gave, and she slumped over her bent knees. She thought of the Beretta in her thigh holster, but Wade second-guessed her intent before she had time to act. "I wouldn't do anything foolish," he warned.

Through the shroud of pain she heard his footsteps, felt his hand brush up against her skin as he reached inside her holster in an effort to relieve her of the temptation a spare weapon might supply. He knew her work habits well.

Wade stuck the confiscated Beretta behind his belt and smoothed out Aya's skirt.

"I'm sorry, I'm so sorry." His hand cradled her cheek. "You left me no choice. I couldn't let you leave. Not this time. You understand, don't you?"

His voice, filled with pity.

His undone shirt collar.

Her knife, lodged in his throat.

Wade's fingers parted from Aya's face, as he clutched at the knife handle. He dropped his gun, fumbled backwards, a gurgle fighting to escape his open mouth, as he choked on his own blood.

Still shaky, Aya scrambled off the ground to pick up the Kimber. "You miserable, hesitant bastard," she whispered, taking aim.

Yet she didn't fire. She only stood there, waiting, watching him fade on his own, and felt nothing. No spite, no sympathy, no regret. Not even relief, only the pain in her shoulder.

And as his body finally went limp, cold reason was the only thing that reigned in her mind.

She unbuttoned her shirt and checked her shoulder. Wade had not hit any major blood vessels, the wound was oozing rather than bleeding profusely. The bullet didn't go through, must have stuck in the shoulder blade. The slug would have to be attended to eventually, but for now Aya's chances of not passing out from blood loss were quite favorable.

She wiped the Kimber thoroughly with her shirt and deposited the weapon into Wade's bloodstained hand. She slipped his Glock into his holster and recovered her Beretta.

"We have to go." She slapped Oishi awake. There was no

time to lose.

With any luck, the cops would think that Wade had been Dannii's killer. And the trace on the Kimber in his hand would only reaffirm their conclusion. Yes, he killed her just before she, forced to drop her own firearm, had hurled the knife that was now stuck in his throat. A very common knife that Aya had used earlier to cut Oishi's tethers. It could have easily belonged to someone like Dannii. And now that its wooden handle was soaked in Wade's blood, no police lab could lift Aya's prints off its surface.

Aya knew there was a possibility that her identity might be discovered, if someone had seen her going into the warehouse for instance. Maltais, for one, could have seen her if he had actually been around. But Maltais wouldn't squawk to the police, not while he knew there was still a chance of recovering the disk. And Wade would have hardly talked to anyone about meeting her, not since she wasn't his primary assignment.

Oishi's blood on the floor might present some difficulty. The police would be stumped, no doubt, as to whom it belonged. Hopefully too stumped to look for the vapors of Aya's own blood. But even if they did tell it apart from the thick layer of dust and grime, that thread was bound to go only nowhere. They would write it off to another unknown suspect who had managed to escape the scene. A further investigation would be conducted, which would produce nothing conclusive.

Wade would receive a nice government-funded funeral, get commended. His parents would cry at his grave. Tieri would blame himself, but not so much as to consider an early retirement. The whole thing would be soon forgotten, faded in everyone's memory like a sand castle fades with each new wave.

IRYNA BENNETT

Life would go on.
The sea would keep its secrets.

ABOUT THE AUTHOR

Iryna Bennett was born in the Ukraine and shuffled through her reasonably conventional formative years with her head buried in books. By the time adolescence rolled around and the scenery settled in around her, she was pleasantly surprised to find herself fresh out of college and residing in Texas. When not writing or being brilliant at her day job, Iryna spends any spare time left over from wardrobe crises taking target practice and adopting felines. *Whoever Fights Monsters* is her first novel.

Lightning Source UK Ltd.
Milton Keynes UK
UKOW06f0624300617
304414UK00015B/897/P